WHAT PEOPLE ARE SAYINE

Rescuing Hope brings the reality of human trafficking to a tangible place where your heart will understand and be compelled to action. Hope, the main character, has become the face of the girls I pray for in Atlanta and around the United States. The prostituted girl no one wants to talk about became my daughter, her cousins, the kids down the street. You'll remember Hope too, long after you put the book down. Don't turn away. Let her move you. Together, we can look evil in the eye and say, "No more!"

PATTIE HARRELSON,
Not for Sale Campaign,
State Director for Georgia

Susan Norris captured my attention and my heart from the very first pages of *Rescuing Hope*. I was immediately drawn so deeply into the story, I couldn't put it down! Full of heartbreak and redemption, this eye-opening, true-to-life novel will not only hold your attention but it will educate you and motivate you to action in the process.

ANNIE DOWNS,
author of *Perfectly Unique* (Zondervan, 2012)
and Girls of Grace speaker

Author Susan Norris superbly captures the essence of child sex trafficking in America. Her compelling story will open your eyes and heart to the horrific truth of what happens on the streets of our country. On behalf of the thousands of voiceless children caught in the net of commercial sexual exploitation, thank you, Susan, for your endurance, perseverance and insight.

BRIAN L. SHIVLER,
CEO, Resolution Hope

RESCUING

HOPE

RESCUING

HOPE

A Story of
Sex Trafficking
in America

SUSAN NORRIS

with April Line

Published in association with Robin Stanley, publishing consultant and author representative. www.robinstanley.org

Manuscript Support: April Line, freelance writer & teacher, www.AprilLineWriting.com
Cover design and photography: Studio Absolute, Russ &
Cheryl McIntosh, www.studioabsolute.com
Author's cover photo: Donna Kay Johnson, www.photographybydonnakay.com
Restoration Song, ©2005, Clay Edwards. Written by: Clay Edwards,
Audra Hartke, and David Brymer. Used by permission.

iUniverse books may be ordered through booksellers or by contacting:
iUniverse
1663 Liberty Drive
Bloomington, IN 47403
www.iuniverse.com
1-800-Authors (1-800-288-4677)

ISBN: 978-1-4759-6623-7 (sc)
ISBN: 978-1-4759-6625-1 (hc)
ISBN: 978-1-4759-6624-4 (e)

Library of Congress Control Number: 2012923078
First Edition 2012
1 2 3 4 5 6 7 8 9 10

Printed in the United States of America
iUniverse rev. date: 12/6/2012

This book is dedicated to the survivors of human sex trafficking, their families, the detectives who rescued them, and the organizations on the front lines who trusted me with their stories. Hope's story is a mixture of your stories. You are my heroes. You're strong and fearless.

ACKNOWLEDGMENTS

I love to read. When I get my hands on a good book, everything else comes to a screeching halt. Never in a million years did I envision myself writing a book. I ran from it as hard and as fast as I could. In many ways, I felt like Jonah running from what God called him to do. In the end, God won out. He always does. This story had to be told. Lives are depending on it.

To the survivors, my heroes, I cannot wait to see how the next chapters in your lives unfold. I am committed to being a voice for the Hopes I've met and those who are still held in bondage.

I thank my husband, Mark, who is my biggest cheerleader and best friend. I wouldn't have had the guts to do this without you. To my children, I love you both and love how you've taken up the cause in your own ways to fight for what is right, even if it means standing alone. To my parents, thank you for teaching me how to be an advocate for others. To my prayer shield, the most amazing group of prayer warriors I know, thank you for always having my back, for pushing me when I needed it and for walking by my side throughout this wild ride. To my agent, Robin Stanley, and my editor, April Line, thank you both for pushing me constantly and stretching me to make this story the best it could be. To Mary Frances Bowley of Wellspring Living, thank you for educating me on the issue, opening doors for me, and encouraging me to write this story. To RiverStone Church, thank you for holding true to the vision of community transformation and challenging us each to find our place in that call. To the staff of the Daily Grind, thank you for allowing me to have a satellite office in your coffee shop to write and process. To Brian Shivler and Resolution Hope, thank you for getting behind this story and spreading the word. Most of all, to my Savior, the Lover of my soul, thank You for allowing me to partner with You in Your work. I'm humbled and amazed by You daily.

To my readers, thank you for taking the time to read about a difficult subject, when it would be easy to turn away. I pray *Rescuing Hope* stirs something inside you to propel you into action. Find your place in the fight against the commercial sexual exploitation of children. There's room for everyone in this battle. We need your voice, your gifts, your talents. What part will you play in becoming a voice for hope?

What you are about to read is fiction. However, the events in this book are based on interviews with survivors of human sex trafficking, their families, detectives, people from religious and rescue organizations on the frontlines, and a former pimp. Some of the content is mature, and though we have strived for a PG-13 treatment of it, this book should be read with adult supervision.

We encourage you to take any questions to an adult you trust.

You may choose to look the other way, but you can never say again that you did not know.
—William Wilberforce

CHAPTER 1

"I need my money." She pulled her tank top back on in the dimly lit room. The scent of their act still hung in the air. She gagged on her shame. Most days she could go through the motions like a robot. But tonight she saw a price tag hanging on her that read "clearance, damaged goods."

"You're nothing," he said. It was like he took a chunk out of her already pulpy soul. The low-watt bulb dangling from the crumbling ceiling was a spotlight that revealed her.

"Pay you! You've got to be kidding me. You weren't worth the time I spent away from my family." He threw her jeans in her face. "Get dressed and get out, you little tramp."

"I can't go back to T without my money." Her voice cracked and rose. She knew T wouldn't take it lightly. "He'll kill me. Then he'll come kill you too."

"I really don't care what he does with you. I'm going to get cleaned up and then I'm out of here. Make sure you're gone when I come out."

The bathroom door closed with a bang. She slid her jeans over her bony hips; she'd always been thin, but this life made her gaunt. Then she saw his wallet on the dresser. She'd pay herself. He wouldn't know until she was long gone. She picked up the wallet and counted out what he owed her just as the water turned off. She put the wallet

1

back exactly where she'd found it, grabbed her shoes and opened the door to leave.

His hand reached over her head and slammed the door shut. His face twisted with rage.

"You little thief!" He grabbed her hands, forcing them open. The money spilled out onto the floor as the color drained from her face.

"Now you're going to pay!"

He threw her up against the wall. His fists crushed into her chin; sour blood slid over her tongue. Stars exploded before her eyes when he grabbed her hair and tossed her to the floor. He unleashed his rage on her, his strength and bulk enfeebling her attempt at fighting back. He wasted her, again. She lay curled on the floor for moments, listening while his breathing slowed. The door opened and signaled the end of his tirade.

"Now get out before I throw you out."

With her last bit of energy, she crawled out the door on her hands and knees. He locked it behind her. She pushed her body into a sitting position and dug in her pocket for something to wipe the blood dripping down her chin. How had this happened? She'd forgotten T's number-one rule: payment before pleasure. She would have to face T's wrath when she showed up without the money, and because bruised doesn't sell. She was stuck. She couldn't turn a trick looking like she did. Her best bet was to get back to the apartment and face what was coming to her.

She made it back to the building but had difficulty finding number twenty-two on the elevator buttons. Her right eye was swollen shut. As the elevator rose, so did her heartbeat. What would T do to her? She knew he wouldn't offer her an ice pack. She began to shiver, even though the elevator was warm.

When she walked in the door, he was talking. On the phone? A girl stood in the doorway to the kitchen, trying to convince him to keep her there instead of sending her out for a job. Hope snuck to the bathroom, she didn't dare turn on the light. A pounding drum had taken up residence in her head. She managed to turn on the water and get undressed. She anticipated relief, but tiny needles penetrated her skin instead. She got out of the bathtub fast, then pulled on sweats she found on the floor.

She'd given up looking at herself in mirrors, except when she applied the heavy makeup T demanded she wear, night after night. Her haircut and color weren't the only changes since she met T. She was dead inside. All that remained was a shell.

Back in the living room, T stood alone, still on the phone. The girl was gone, probably off to collect what mattered most to him . . . money. T would sell his own mother if the price were right.

She walked out on the balcony for a smoke while T was distracted. Cigarettes were just one of the many coping mechanisms she'd acquired. Her hand trembled as she lifted the cigarette to her lips. Her heartbeat sounded like a jackhammer in her own ears. T would be beyond furious.

As she flicked her cigarette over the balcony, she shivered, sensing T behind her. Answer time. She turned. His jaw dropped.

"What the hell happened to you?"

She knew better than to pull away from him, but his volume sent her head spinning.

"I asked the guy to pay me, but he said I was going to pay. He left his calling card on my face." Her legs were shaking so hard, she didn't know if they would hold her up. T got violent when people ripped him off.

"He did this to you before you did the job?" He stepped back and started pacing.

"No," she almost whispered. "When I got there he started moving fast. He said I was late. I wasn't late, T. You know. You dropped me off. I didn't have time to get the money beforehand. I know I messed up, T. Please don't be angry with me. Please."

T didn't say another word, which scared her. Her body trembled. He stormed into the apartment smacking the glass door as he went. It cracked. He opened a cabinet and pulled out a couple of guns and a knife. He yelled down the hall, "Get up, Rick! We got a score to settle."

Her heart raced as she looked out over the city. Just as her breathing started to settle, he came up behind her again. This time he grabbed her, having no concern for her injuries, and dangled her over the balcony by her feet.

"No! T, please! Please don't drop me! I'm sorry! I promise I won't ever do it again. I'll always get the money first. I promise. God, please don't drop me!" She choked back tears. "I promise. Please!"

"Don't you ever show up after a job without my money! You hear me? If you do, I'll drop you and you'll be replaced before you even hit the ground. You got it, bitch?"

She nodded as he let her fall in a heap on the balcony floor and stormed back inside. Her body wracked with sobs as T yelled, "Let's roll!"

She clung to the sliding glass door for support as Rick came in the room, pulling his shirt on. "What the hell?" He stared at her.

"We ain't got time for this," T said. "We got a score to settle." He tossed Rick one of the guns. "Some prick did this and sent her home without money. I'm gonna kill his ass. Don't nobody mess with my money!" He rushed out ahead of Rick. Rick followed with a glance back before the door closed.

CHAPTER 2

Eighteen months earlier

The door to the choir room burst open, startling Hope Ellis. She needed a minute to settle her nerves.

"You won't believe it, Hope. The place is filling up faster than last year." Sydney Clarkston's words flew out of her mouth. "They've already started seating people in the overflow room."

"So much for a moment of peace and quiet."

Youth Sunday was one of Hope's favorites. She had butterflies in her stomach as they approached the sanctuary. Hope and Sydney had been best friends since they were little, and today they were going to sing "Restoration." Everyone said their duets were angelic. "I can't believe we're finally going to sing this song. I think it's my all-time favorite." Hope threw her arm around Sydney as they headed onto stage.

The praise band took their places on the raised platform in the front of the sanctuary wearing T-shirts that read "Rocking with the Rock!" Hope and Sydney had bedazzled theirs with rhinestones and puff paint, and the lights shone off their sparkles as they took their places.

When the band was ready, they began to sing, "You bring restoration, You bring restoration, You bring restoration to my soul."

The congregation joined the song; some of them held their palms up in praise. The first time Hope heard the song, she felt like it was written for her alone. As people spilled into the front of the Moriah Church for prayer, she realized the song resonated with other people too. After they sang the last chorus, Hope and Sydney continued to play softly. Hope knew God would take the shattered pieces of those kneeling and put them back together.

After the service, the youth group moved like a caffeinated herd while they made plans for a celebratory lunch. Hope's mom grabbed her from behind. "Hey, you! I am so proud of you. You and Sydney sounded amazing. That song makes me cry every time I hear you sing it."

"Me too, Mom. I barely made it through without losing it." Hope hugged her mom. Though her dad had been gone for two years, she was still raw over it. But the divorce had knit her and her mom tighter than ever.

"Can I go out with the gang? I won't be late. I still have to finish my research paper."

"Sure, but homework isn't the only thing waiting for you. We have to start packing too. Be home by three." Hope's mom gave her a kiss on the forehead.

"I wish we didn't have to move. I don't want to change schools."

"I know, sweetheart, but there isn't another option. The last time I looked, we didn't have a money tree in the backyard."

What would it be like in their new house? Who would she hang out with? She sure couldn't run across town every day after school. She and Sydney were only fourteen. At least she'd be able to spend most of her summer with Syd.

After a spirited lunch with her youth group, and some bittersweet parting words—she really did feel like she was leaving the planet—she ran in her front door at two fifty-five.

"Mom, I'm home!" No answer. She walked through the house. "Mom?"

Her mom paced on the patio, talking on the phone. Her hair looked a little messy, and she was slicing the air in front of her with her free hand. She'd changed into her stained jeans and a T-shirt to start packing and cleaning.

"Are you serious? We can't reschedule the moving company. What am I going to do?" Hope's mom was typically mild. Even when she grounded Hope, it was done with love. But all the stress she'd been under made her a little touchy sometimes. Hope had learned it was better to just stay out of her mom's way at times like those.

She gathered her things for her research paper while her mom finished. Hope didn't even hear her mom come into the den.

"Hey, honey. Gram called. Pops fell and he's messed up his knee. It's not serious, but Gram will have to stay home and take care of him and help him get around, so they're not going to be able to help us move. Maybe my new boss will let me take a day off."

"Mom, that's ridiculous."

"What choice do I have?"

"I'm old enough to handle it. What's so hard about watching the movers take stuff out of one house and put it in another house? I'll see if Mrs. Clarkston can give me a ride to the new house when they're done or I'll just ride in the truck with the movers. We're paying them enough; they shouldn't mind."

"It would be nice if I didn't have to ask for a day off work my first week, but I'm not sure I'm comfortable leaving you."

"Mom, I'll be fine. The Clarkstons are across the street and Syd can hang out with me. What could go wrong?"

"You're right. I'll call the movers and let them know. Now, get on that term paper. It's not going to write itself."

* * *

Hope woke to her mom screaming, "Where is it? I don't have time for this."

Hope scrambled to her mom's bedroom door. "Where's what?" She leaned against the doorjamb, yawning.

"My hairbrush . . . I can't find my hairbrush. How am I supposed to start a new job with my hair looking like this?" She pointed to the tangled mess on her head.

"You can use my hairbrush. I'm sure yours will turn up when we unpack."

Her mom followed her and picked up her hairbrush. She kissed the top of Hope's head as she climbed back into bed. "Sorry I woke you. This job wasn't easy to get, and I don't want to lose it on the first day."

"You're gonna be fine, Mom. They're not going to fire you because of your hair." She pulled the covers up. "Call me at lunchtime and let me know how it's going."

"You won't be home. You and Sydney will be running around having too much fun to think about me and my job."

"Ummm, hello, cell phone." She waved her new cell phone in the air.

"You slept with it? Good grief, I don't understand teenagers. Have a good day, honey. I love you!"

"Love you too." Hope drifted back to sleep.

CHAPTER 3

On moving day, Hope's mom woke her up at seven. "This is not right! It's the second day of summer vacation and I'm awake before God turned the lights on."

"Wait a minute. I offered to ask off from work, but you assured me you were old enough to handle it. You can't back out now. I've got to leave in thirty minutes and I need you up and dressed before I go."

"I know, I know. I'll do it. I said I would and I meant it. I just wish they could start the job later in the day." She tried to burrow deeper under the covers, but her mom pulled them off. "Fat chance! If they start any later, they'll be moving stuff after dark."

"Hey!" The air on her legs was too cold for summer. No wonder Hope hated mornings. She felt the bed shift as her mom sat down next to her. She snuggled closer to her mom seeking warmth and sighed in comfort as her mom's nails moved over her back. Hope sat up reluctantly.

Hope's mom stood up, "You've got the key, right?"

"Yes, I have the key. And your work phone number. And the number for the real estate agent in case there is a problem." Hope stood up and stretched. "I'm going to be fine. Stop worrying about me. You need to worry about your hair. I think you need my hairbrush again."

"Very cute, missy. Don't be mean just because it's the morning. Now get in the shower so you're finished before I leave. I'm going to see if I can find anything other than packing tape for breakfast."

In a matter of minutes, Hope walked into the kitchen where her mom stared at her. "Why aren't you dressed?"

"I am dressed. What's the point of dirtying anything up just to sit around and read a book while these guys work? It's not like I'm gonna see anyone."

"Whatever. The guys' names are Troy and James. They'll be driving a blue moving van, but it doesn't have a logo on it yet. They're still fighting about whose name goes first. I hope I remember to drive to the new house tonight."

"You'll be fine, Mom. Don't worry about a thing. If I have any questions, I can always call Mrs. Clarkston to come over and help me."

"They're driving up to Asbury today, remember? I think it's a little early for Sydney to be looking at colleges, but better early than late, I guess. They won't be home after lunch time. Just call me at work if you need me."

Hope rolled her eyes. "Yeah. I mean, we haven't even started high school yet. I can't imagine looking at colleges. Thanks for not being nuts about college visits yet."

"Who do you think you're kidding? You're absolutely going to college."

"Yeah, in four years."

Hope gave her mom a kiss good-bye and handed her her coffee.

Hope's mom blew the horn as she backed out, causing Hope to jump. "Call me if you need me. Love you!"

* * *

James and Troy were right on time. They looked to be in their early twenties. James was in charge; at least, he did most of the talking. He was about six feet tall, with blond hair and killer blue eyes. Troy seemed a little taller and had small green eyes that cut right through Hope. He was bald and beefy with cryptic tattoos peeking out of his T-shirt's neckline. He looked like a gym nut. When he looked at her, it was creepy, like he was checking her out. She avoided him all day.

James told Hope they'd pack the living room last so she would have somewhere to sit and relax while they worked. He even mentioned they wouldn't disconnect the television until they were ready to load it. He was friendly. The two guys were opposites. Maybe Troy was just the quiet type. She'd give him the benefit of the doubt.

Late in the morning, Sydney and her mom walked over with sandwiches for Hope and the movers.

"It's the least we can do since we're leaving you here by yourself." Mrs. Clarkston handed Hope the bag. "Now you tell your mom that once you're settled in the new house, we'll bring dinner and we want the grand tour. I love you, sweet girl. See you soon."

"Thanks, Mrs. Clarkston. Love you too!"

"Sydney, you've got ten minutes before your dad will be ready to go. It's not like you guys won't ever see each other again. Hope's coming over next week for a sleepover, so don't keep us waiting."

"Yes, ma'am."

"Bye, Mrs. Clarkston. Thanks for lunch."

"You're welcome, Hope. See you soon."

"Call me when you get back from Asbury." Hope drew her BFF into a bear hug.

"Call you. What are you talking about? I'm gonna be texting you the whole way there and back now that you have a cell phone." Hope tried to break their embrace. "Excuse me, I'm not done hugging!"

When Sydney finally drew back, her eyes were a little red. Hope said, "See you in a few days? Tell your mom thanks again for lunch."

Hope went into the kitchen with her lunch as Troy and James finished eating. "Thanks, little lady, for the lunch. It was nice of you to take care of us." Troy brushed by her.

"You're welcome." Hope stepped aside. That guy gave her the creeps.

James thanked her on his way back to work.

"We're going to load up the living room while you're eating lunch. Then we'll throw the kitchen table in the back and head to your new house." James put her book on the kitchen counter.

"Okay."

They worked fast. As she took her last bite, they came for the kitchen table.

"You might want to walk through to make sure we didn't miss anything," Troy said. "We don't want to have to come back."

Hope walked through the house. She'd lived there since she was born. All of her childhood memories were there. If her dad hadn't left, they'd still be able to live here, like a real family. She shook off the memories. The movers were waiting.

She'd have to make memories in a new house. Closing the door behind her, she climbed in the moving truck beside James.

"You got it all. Let's go."

The new house was a lot smaller, and the guys unloaded quickly.

At five o'clock, James hooked up the television while Troy finished assembling her bed. They were almost done. Hope would be glad to have the house to herself till her mom got home at six thirty. She planned to find the linens and surprise her mom by making the beds.

Troy took their carpet covers out to the truck while James brought her the paperwork to sign.

"Thanks for all your help."

"No problem." James folded the check and put it in his shirt pocket. "Make sure you tell all of your friends about JT Moving Company."

"You mean TJ Moving Company," Troy called from the sidewalk.

"Thanks, ya'll." Hope couldn't deal with the quiet while she looked for the sheets, so she dug her iPod out from her purse and blasted tobyMac in her ears. When she carried her sheets into her room, she noticed that Troy had left a screwdriver and one of those L-shaped wrenches on the carpet by the bed.

Hope made her mom's bed first, then went back to her room. The top sheet snapped in the air then fell on her bed as she danced to the side of it to pull the sheet tight. The doorbell startled her; its echo between the walls was strange. Puzzled, Hope made her way to the front door.

CHAPTER 4

Hope paused. "Who is it?"

"It's Troy. I left some tools when I put the beds together."

Looking out the window, she saw a blue Ford pickup truck in her driveway instead of the moving truck. When she opened the door, Troy stood on the porch alone with his hands in his pockets.

"Just a minute, I'll get them for you." She turned to walk down the hall.

"Thanks. James will kill me if I lose his tools."

As Hope bent over to retrieve the tools, the hair on the back of her neck stood up. She turned around and was surprised to see Troy filling the doorway. Hadn't she told him to wait?

"How do you like your new room?"

Hope shifted from foot to foot, not sure what to do. He should've stayed on the porch.

"Um, it's fine." She took a step toward the door, offering him the tools. He didn't move to take the tools. He didn't step away from the door. Hope's heart beat so loudly in her ears she was sure he could hear it.

"Excuse me." She tried to get past him but felt suffocated by his presence. He stood there like a steel door.

"You know, I saw you checking me out when we were here earlier." His cocky grin made her shiver.

"What?" Her voice cracked. "I was not checking you out. I was reading my book."

"Like hell you weren't. I'm not stupid." He took a step toward her. "I came back to give you a better look, up close and personal."

Hope took a step back and scanned the room for her cell phone. It was across the room on her desk. She was trapped. Her legs began to tremble. She clutched her hands tightly around the tools, trying to think. *Mom, please come home early.*

Troy reached out and pulled Hope against him pressing the tools between them as he planted his lips on hers in a forceful kiss. She struggled to pull away but he was too strong. Pushing on his chest was like pushing on a brick wall.

"No need to play-hard-to-get, sweetheart, I know you've been thinking about this all day."

She tried to scream, but he clamped his big hand over her mouth as he pushed her onto the bed. His finger felt like sandpaper under her nose. He straddled her. *The screwdriver!* She tried to stab him in the ribs. Unfazed, he used his free hand and legs to pin her to the bed.

"How sweet, you made the bed up for us and everything." He laughed.

Tears streamed down her face as he pulled her sweatpants off and began to have his way. She felt sick from the burn of his thrusts. Snot, sweat, and tears collected on his hand while she wriggled and fought with all of her might. "Get off of me, you animal!" she screamed against his hand. No one heard her. She tried to bite him, but when she breathed in through her nose, she coughed. Hoping to push him off of her, she thrashed her legs, but he was so much bigger than she was. The more she fought, the more brutal he became.

Trying to block out the pain, she squeezed her eyes shut, hoping to disappear. He finished and stood up. She heard him pull his jeans back up and zip them. Trembling, she refused to open her eyes and curled into a ball in a futile effort to protect herself. Maybe it was a bad dream, she would open her eyes and be back in her old room with her mom making breakfast downstairs.

She'd almost convinced herself it was a nightmare when she heard Troy's voice. She winced.

"This is our little secret. You wanted it as bad as I did. I saw it in your eyes. Now be a good girl and clean up this mess before your mom gets home. If you tell anyone, I'll come back and do it again. And next time, I'll do it to your mom too."

She heard him pick up the tools, then the latch to the front door fall into place. She wanted to die. What had she done to deserve this? Did she look at him differently than she did James? Did she accidentally give him the wrong idea? It was her fault. She'd insisted on helping her mom with the movers. Why did they have to move? Her body continued to quake, her gut dropped as her cell phone buzzed. Too late. She managed to get to her desk. Mom.

On my way home.

Why now? Why couldn't she have come home sooner—before Troy showed up?

Hope couldn't tell her mom what happened. It was too risky. Troy would come back and hurt them both. She pulled the sheets off the bed, the tangy waft of sweat and Troy hit her sinuses and made her dizzy. There was a little bit of blood. Was it hers? What if she was really bleeding. She'd have to tell her mom it was her period. She couldn't bear to look at herself. How would she ever be able to sleep there? She dropped the sheets on the floor and kicked them under the bed until she could get rid of them forever. She had to shower. Maybe soap and hot water would wash Troy off of her, wash the shame away. She scrubbed her mouth until her lips felt bruised, tried to wipe off the feeling of Troy's lips on hers. She had never even kissed a boy before.

Her mom said sex was a beautiful wedding gift to give only to your spouse. She was ruined forever. There was no gift to give. She scrubbed until it hurt. Sobbed and scrubbed. She felt more nauseous by the minute. Her stomach emptied itself violently. She opened the drain to wash the vomit down and scrubbed even harder. She turned the water off, and heard her mom call out. "Hope, I'm home! Where are you?"

"I'm in the bathroom." How would she explain her puffy eyes? Her mom would notice instantly and begin asking questions. Her phone buzzed. It was a text from Sydney.

About halfway. How's ur new house? Do u love ur room?

Sydney . . . she would be Hope's excuse for the puffy eyes. Her mom would believe she was crying because of their good-bye.

Hope jumped as her mom tapped on the door. She didn't know how long she'd been standing there.

"Hope? Are you all right in there?"

"Yeah, I'm coming."

Hope walked out of the bathroom in her robe.

"Sweetheart, have you been crying?"

Hope bristled. *Don't call me sweetheart. Don't ever call me sweetheart again. There's nothing sweet about me anymore.*

"I'm fine, Mom. It hit me when the movers left. We've really moved. I won't live across the street from Sydney ever again." Hope's voice sounded tinny and strained. She began crying again. Her mom wrapped her up in a hug.

"Oh, Hope. I'm so, so sorry."

Hope felt safe. She held on tight. She followed her mom around the house all night asking if she was sure the doors were locked. "Do you think we could get a security system?"

"Security system? Why on earth would we need a security system? We've never had one before."

"I felt safer in our old house. I knew everyone there and Sydney was always across the street. I don't know the people here and I'd just feel safer if we could get one."

"I'll look into it. It depends on how much it costs. Even though I started a new job, I'm not making what I used to make. We've got to get a handle on our bills before we can add additional expenses.

Hope unpacked box after box; the monotony of the work was comforting. She could get lost in piling linens in the closet and putting her shirts in drawers one by one. Imagining her room as her old room wasn't so hard when all she looked at was her old dresser. She almost jumped out of her skin when she heard her mom's voice from the other room. "Hope? I'm pooped. I'm going to hop in the shower. Let's go to bed early so we can get an early start tomorrow."

"Can I come in and hear about your day?" Hope emerged from her tainted room, heading for the living room where her mom finished alphabetizing DVDs.

"You haven't done that in ages."

"I know, Mom, but Sydney's not here to talk to and you just started a new job, and we're living in a new house and—"

"Okay, okay, suit yourself."

After her mom was in her pajamas, Hope paced in front of her bed. "Would you mind if I sleep in here with you?"

"What in the world is going on? You've been acting strange all night. Is everything all right?"

"No, Mom, everything is not all right! You made me move away from my home, away from my best friend in the whole world, and you brought me here where I don't know anyone. I don't have any friends and I hate it! I hate this house! I hate my life! I hate it!"

"Hope!" Her mom wrapped Hope in her arms. "You were fine this morning when I left and now you act like your whole world has been turned upside down. What went wrong?"

"Everything, Mom. Everything!"

"You can sleep with me tonight. But you're going to have to sleep in your own room tomorrow. Things will get better. You'll see."

Hope climbed into her mom's bed and tried to sleep, but every time she closed her eyes, she saw Troy.

CHAPTER 5

Hope couldn't make herself sleep in her own bed. She could hardly dress in there. She started watching movies late at night so she could sleep on the sofa. Her mom believed she fell asleep in the middle of the movie. Sometimes she left the television on with the volume down to make her story more plausible. When her mom questioned her, Hope's reply was always the same, "Mom, this is what you do when you're in high school."

Sydney continued to text Hope from Asbury.

Hope, wat sup? U don't seem like urself.

"While you were riding to Asbury with your family, I was raped by one of the movers. Other than that, I'm fabulous," sounded terrible. She wanted to talk through it with someone. Her stomach was in knots. She didn't keep secrets from Sydney or her mom. She was living in the prison of her mind, isolated and wanting to die.

Hard time adjusting. Will b fine. Just going 2 take time.

B home n a few daz. Sleepover my house. U can tell me all about it.

Fat chance.

Can't wait.

Hope would have to perform for everyone, give them the answers they expected. No one could know the truth.

That weekend Hope knew her mom would do everything in her power to get Hope out of her funk. If only she could tell her mom everything. It wouldn't make it go away, but maybe she could move forward instead of being stuck.

Hope loved to get lost in a book. When she read, she didn't have to face her world. She could step into another time and place and stay there as long as she wanted. Yet she couldn't finish the book she was reading on moving day. It had been on the kitchen counter since then.

"Can you take me to the bookstore to get some new books, Mom?"

"You haven't even finished the book you were reading."

"I know. It's hard to get into and I just don't feel like investing anymore time in it if it isn't any good."

"We have to tighten our belts for a while until I see how far my paycheck goes. Why don't we go to the library? It's filled with books I won't have to store. I'm surprised the movers didn't throw their backs out moving all of your books."

At the mention of the movers, Hope tensed and the sting of bile rose in her throat. "Whatever, Mom." She rushed to the bathroom. *God, how am I going to do this? I'm so alone.* She slid down the bathroom wall to the floor.

My daughter, you are never alone. I will never leave you nor forsake you.

Hope couldn't believe it. "Never leave me nor forsake me? Where were You when I was being raped, God? Where were You then? You weren't there! You did forsake me! In fact, I don't know why I'm even talking to You. It's not like You really care; if You did, this would have never happened."

There was a knock on the door. "Hope, did you say something?"

"Just talking to myself."

"Are you all right?"

"Yeah, don't worry."

At least she could count on her mom. But her mom wasn't always around, which meant Hope had to come up with another solution.

* * *

They pulled up to the curb at the library. "I'm going to run to the grocery store for a few things and then I'll be right back, so you don't have long. I'll text you when I get back."

"Okay, see you in a few."

This branch of the library looked older than the one by her old house, not that she had frequented it. She usually bought books. She liked to stay connected to the worlds she visited. Reading was one of her coping mechanisms when her parents starting having problems. It helped her to escape the fighting. But she loved the smell in the library, the mildly musky old paper smell mixed with ink and electricity. This library still had a card catalog. Hope went up to it.

"I don't think you'll find anything in there," an older woman with short, graying, permed hair said.

Hope was startled, "Really? Why is it here?"

"I couldn't bring myself to get rid of it when they went digital. It's here for nostalgia. But only about half of the books here are in there."

Hope stuck her hand out. "I'm Hope Ellis."

"You can call me Ms. Joyce."

"Nice to meet you."

"Enjoy the stacks."

Hope didn't have a particular book or author in mind. She just knew she needed an escape. She waited for something to grab her attention as she strolled the aisles. When she got to the Ms in Fiction, she saw a person of interest. He looked a couple of years older than she was. He seemed confident. Hiding behind a book on the same aisle, she continued to study him over it. He was tall and thin, but not too thin. His dark hair looked intentionally shaggy. He whispered to someone through the stacks, but Hope couldn't see who. Probably his girlfriend.

Just as she put the book away, she saw him slide something through the stacks to the other person, and when he pulled his hand back, he had money in it. He quickly counted it, then shoved it in his pocket—and looked up.

Caught, she tried to play it off. Their eyes locked and he smiled, pulling another book off the shelf. He turned to go. He glanced over his shoulder at her as he passed. He tossed the book aside and made his way out the door.

Her pocket vibrated.

`I'm here. Let's go before the ice cream melts. I got strawberry sorbet.`

Hope smiled. Her mom used perfect grammar and punctuation in her texts. Only parents did that.

She walked to the door. As she pushed it open, out of the corner of her eye she noticed a girl looking at her from the stacks. Hope stared at the library door as she climbed in the car.

"What? No books?"

"No, I didn't have a lot of time to look. I might come back tomorrow."

Sydney would be home tomorrow. Hope wasn't sure how she would keep Sydney from pestering her with questions. She was bound to pick up on Hope's gray state. That was tomorrow's problem. She had to get through tonight without sleeping in her room. Suddenly Hope had an idea.

"Hey, Mom, we haven't had a girls' night in a long time. I think we need to break the new house in with an all-night movie fest, complete with popcorn and candy for dinner. Can we?"

"Oh, honey, I'm beat. Can we do it another time?"

"Please? Tomorrow night I'm gonna be at Sydney's. This is the perfect night to do it, just you and me. Please!"

"Oh, all right. I guess I can take a nap tomorrow if I need to. Let's drop the groceries off and we'll go rent some movies. But you have to promise you'll help me unpack a few boxes tomorrow before you head to Sydney's."

"You got it!"

Hope steered clear of the romance movies to which she typically gravitated. She couldn't handle watching any kind of love story. She went for what her mom called the oldies but goodies and chose *Parent Traps 1* and *2*, *Finding Nemo*, and *Freaky Friday*.

Once they got home, Hope took a shower. She still threw up every time she got in there. It became comforting; it was her only way to purge. The smell of popcorn greeted her when she opened the door, and she almost forgot, almost.

Her mom made a tray of finger sandwiches to go along with their junk food.

"What's wrong, Mom, couldn't survive on Raisinettes, Coke, and popcorn?"

"I'm a mom, remember, not a high school student. Plus, it won't kill us to eat something with nutritional value, will it?" Climbing over Hope's outstretched legs, she got comfortable.

"Hey, we're eating raisins that happen to be covered in dark chocolate. Doctors say dark chocolate is a superfood." Hope's side hurt from laughing at her own joke. She nudged close to her mom on the sofa, she pressed play on the DVD remote. She felt safe.

Her nose stung with the sentimental tears she always cried when Nemo and his dad reunited, and Hope cried real tears at the memory of when she was carefree, when the most intense thing on her mind was whether to wear skinny jeans or a skirt. Tonight she chose to live in happily-ever-after land, even if it was a fairy tale.

Hope woke up to the smell of bacon cooking. She was still on the sofa, covered in a blanket. How she wished she could escape that easily every day. Hope wasn't sure she'd ever feel truly happy again. She stifled a yawn as she wandered into the kitchen. Her mom pulled the pan of bacon out of the microwave.

"Good morning—or should I say good afternoon?"

"What time is it?" Hope stretched her arms high above her head as she yawned again.

"Past noon, Sleepyhead. Why don't you sit down so I can get some food in you before Sydney shows up to take you away. So much for you helping me unpack."

"Sorry. I really intended to help you." She crammed bacon in her mouth. "I gotta get ready. Can I just make a bacon biscuit for the road so Syd and Mrs. Clarkston don't have to wait for me?"

"Sure, and make one for Sydney too."

Hope ran to her room and threw on shorts and a T-shirt, then grabbed her things and crammed them in a backpack as the doorbell rang. Every time she went into her room, she felt like she was running a marathon, trying to get out before any of the ick settled onto her skin, before any of the memories could assault her.

"Hey, Syd! How was Asbury?" Her mom led Sydney into the kitchen.

"It's awesome." Sydney beamed. "It is such a beautiful campus."

Hope came down the hall.

"Hey, you!" Sydney said. "Are you ready? I'm dying to tell you all about our trip and the cute guys I saw. You think high school is going to be great. College looks a-maz-ing!" Sydney did a little dance of excitement.

It was comfortable being with Sydney, but Hope wondered what her friend would say if she knew the truth.

Hope gave her mom a kiss. "Are you sure you're okay being in the house alone?"

"Why on earth wouldn't I be?"

"Make sure you lock the doors. We don't know the neighbors yet."

"I'm fine, Hope. You've been watching too many movies or something." Her mom gave her a hug. "Have fun and I'll see you tomorrow."

Sydney and Hope piled into the back seat of Mrs. Clarkston's Prius, and Syd didn't take a breath the whole way to her house. Hope couldn't think of much to say. She couldn't stop worrying about her mom being in the house by herself. What if Troy came back and found her mom there alone? Would she be safe?

"Are you even listening to me?" Sydney poked her.

"Sure I am. You were telling me how you learned all about John Wesley on the tour."

"Yeah, five minutes ago. What's with you, Hopester? You're not yourself,"

"Not awake yet, I guess." She faked a yawn. "I'm sorry. Start over."

"Never mind; it wasn't important. I'm saving the good stuff for when we don't have big ears around." She pointed to the front seat.

CHAPTER 6

Hope didn't make it through the sleepover at Sydney's house. Poor Mrs. Clarkston had to drive her home at eleven after she lost her dinner in their toilet. She couldn't tell them it was because she caught the phantom scent of Troy. She had to fake real sickness or the Clarkstons would think she was bulimic. If only. She had to come up with another plan for being away from her house all summer. Then it dawned on her. The library. That Ms. Joyce seemed nice, and Hope did love books.

"Mom, how would you feel about me doing some volunteer work at the library this summer?"

Hope's mother turned the sink off and turned to her. "Slow down, kiddo! Are you feeling better this morning?"

"Yeah. Must've been a little bug."

"I'm glad you're better. Do you feel up to anything for breakfast?"

"Mom, I asked you first. What about the library?"

"I think that's a great plan! How do you know there's an opening?"

"I saw a sign when we stopped by the other day." It was the first time she had ever blatantly lied to her mom, but she was desperate. Hope knew Sydney would see through her excuses and eventually pry the truth out of her. That would put her and her mom at risk.

"Okay, let's stop by this afternoon after church. You can fill out an application. Now what do you want for breakfast?"

"Thanks, Mom. I guess I'll just make myself some cereal." Now all she had to do was convince the librarian.

"I'm glad you're finally making an effort to embrace our new home." Her mom finished clearing her breakfast dishes. "Hurry up and eat, then go get dressed before we're late."

Hope didn't think she could sit through the service. She felt like such a phony. First she had been ruined by Troy and now she was lying to her mother.

As they pulled in the parking lot, Hope saw Sydney standing by the front door, waiting for her. Hope willed herself out of the car. Sydney would detect something if she took too long. It was odd how she could feel trapped while standing outside in the open. The closer she got to the front door, the harder it was to breathe. She couldn't make herself walk into the sanctuary. That was God's house, where truth dwelled. The giggles coming from a nearby minivan gave her an idea.

"Hey, Syd, let's see if they need any help in the nursery today. It's been forever since we've done that. It'll be fun!"

"Works for me."

After church, Hope told Sydney she had to run. "I'm going to see about a volunteer position at the library. That way I can read all day long, and I won't have to buy a single book."

"Good luck," Sydney yelled. "I hope you get it."

Guilt crept up Hope's neck as she made her way to the car. Her emotions were playing tug-of-war. She plastered a smile on her face, took a deep breath, and climbed in the front seat.

When they arrived at the library, Hope's mom started to get out of the car. "Mom, you can't come in with me. It'll look like I'm some little girl who can't do anything without her mommy. I'm just going inside to see if the position is still available. If it is, then I'll fill out an application."

"Okay, Big Girl, I'll wait right here, but don't take too long. I'm hungry."

The library seemed empty. A huge stack of books sat on the cart needing to be shelved. She couldn't find the librarian anywhere. She decided to demonstrate her usefulness and started putting the books away. A few minutes later, Ms Joyce emerged from the back office.

"Hope, was it? Can I help you?" She looked over her glasses.

"Actually, I can help you. I love to read and I love being around books. I noticed you have a lot of work to do and not a lot of help. I was wondering if I could come by each day and do some volunteer work. It would help me earn my scouting badge." She felt her voice going up an octave as she said the last thing. It was how she used to talk to her mom when she was trying to convince her to let her get ice cream. It surprised Hope how easy lying was getting. She was desperate—and desperate circumstances called for desperate measures, right?

"How many hours do you need for your badge?"

"I would like to help each day if I could, for a few hours. You don't have to pay me. You don't even have to fill out a lot of paperwork."

"When do you need to start?"

"I can be here tomorrow morning."

"Great. I'll see you then."

Hope smiled. Finally, something worked in her favor. With a skip in her step she made her way out to the car.

"What on earth took you so long?"

"It takes a while to have an interview."

"She interviewed you on the spot?"

"Yep! And I got the job. I start tomorrow morning and work every day, five days a week."

"Honey, that's a lot of hours. Are you sure you want to do that? It won't leave you much time to hang out with Sydney. This is summer."

"I know, but I thought it would be a way to meet kids I'll go to school with who share my interests. Plus"—Hope leaned forward excitedly—"I can read all the books I want without having to buy a single one!"

"Hm." Her mother looked thoughtful. "If you're sure—"

"And you won't have to worry about me being in the house alone," Hope said.

"Promise me you'll tell me if this gets to be too much for you."

"I promise." Hope hugged her mother.

Up and dressed bright and early the next morning, Hope was making sandwiches when her mom came in to fix a cup of coffee. "You're up mighty early."

"I thought I'd pack us both a lunch. It will save us money and it's my way of saying 'thank you' to you for allowing me to do this volunteer job. I'm really excited about it."

"I'm proud of you. You're really growing up now that you're in high school. Do you have your things together?"

"All I have to do is brush my teeth and then we can go."

Hope was waiting in the car when her mom walked out the front door. She wanted to make certain her days of staying home alone in the house were over.

When she arrived at the library, Ms. Joyce had a cart of books waiting for her to shelve.

"Good morning, Ms. Joyce. Are these books all ready to go?"

"Yes, dear. Bring your things into the office and then you can get started."

Hope wanted to make herself invaluable to Ms. Joyce, so she wasted no time getting started. By lunchtime Hope had shelved three carts full of books.

When she went to ask Ms. Joyce what she could do next, she spotted the guy from the other day. "Do you know that guy over there?"

"I'm not into matchmaking, Miss Ellis." She looked sternly at Hope.

"Oh, no ma'am, I'm not interested in him that way. I noticed him in here the other day and I wondered about him, because he didn't leave with a book."

"Funny you should say that. He's been here a lot, and I've never noticed that before. But you're right. Maybe he's meeting someone. A lot of people meet in the library. It was a very popular meeting place before Starbucks opened."

"Really?"

"Yes, really."

"What should I do next?"

"I'm all out of jobs, Hope. Maybe find a book and read a bit?"

Ms. Joyce didn't have to ask Hope twice.

Hope kept an eye on the guy, trying to see who he met. When she rounded the corner to look for something to read, she saw the same girl she'd seen before. She looked to be about Hope's age, but a little taller. Hope wanted to know what was going on. She placed the books on the shelf and then turned to the girl. "Can I help you find anything?"

"You?" The girl looked surprised. "What? Do you, like, work here or something?"

"Yeah, I do. Are you looking for a particular book?"

Hope noticed the girl looking over her shoulder at the door. When she looked too, she saw the guy leaving quickly.

"Did I interrupt something?"

"No, my friend was just leaving." The girl seemed nervous but also curious. "How old are you? You don't look old enough to be a librarian. You look my age."

"How old are *you*?" Hope couldn't believe the girl's boldness.

The girl put her hand on her hip. "I'm fourteen. I'm going into high school this fall."

"I'm fourteen too. I'm just volunteering here. I really like books."

The girl laughed. "Wow, I didn't know anyone our age really liked to read books. My name is Nikki." She stuck out her hand.

Hope took her offered hand and shook it. "I'm Hope. So why do you keep coming to the library if you don't like books?"

"I meet my friend Blake here. I know him from school, and we like to hang out sometimes. Is there a rule against that?"

"Not that I know of. I think you can be here as long as you want."

"Sweet! Well, I gotta roll. I'll catch you later."

"Yeah, sure, later." As Nikki strolled out of the library, Hope wondered about her story.

CHAPTER 7

That Friday night, Sydney and Hope finally got together. Sydney's mom drove them to the movies, and they were planning to see *High School Musical 3*. Ms. Joyce had given Hope a pair of movie tickets for all her hard work. Hope was proud to be treating, even though she couldn't afford popcorn or anything.

"Let's go to Johnny's," Sydney's mom suggested when she saw the sign.

The girls agreed, and she eased her Prius into the parking lot. A car behind them honked.

"What's the big hurry?" Sydney's mom said, to nobody in particular.

"You don't have to stop before you turn right, Mom."

"I didn't!" She coasted into a parking spot next to a blue Ford pickup, and Hope froze. What if it was Troy's truck? She would lose it if she had to face him.

"Are you coming?" Sydney knocked on the window. Hope realized she was still sitting in the car.

"Sorry, I just zoned out."

Hope walked between them and put her arms through both of their arms. At least this way she would be surrounded. They asked for a table for three. Hope looked around while the waitress grabbed some menus.

Sydney followed her gaze. "Are you looking for anyone in particular?"

"Oh, nope, just wanted to see who was here. It's been a while, you know."

Hope's heart rate slowed as they walked to their table. Troy wasn't there. It must have been someone else's truck. She needed to shift her mind off of him and back onto her friends.

After Mrs. Clarkston dropped off the girls at the theater, they chose seats in the back row for dancing and singing along with "Right Here, Right Now" and "Walk Away." As the theater filled up, Hope thought she spotted the girl, Nikki, from the library. That was odd. Did she live on this side of town? The theater lights went down and the music started. For the next two hours, Hope was lost in the energy and music, worry free.

Sydney talked nonstop about the movie on the ride home, telling her mother every detail. Hope realized how much she missed her friend. Sydney's zest for life was contagious. Once Syd finished her debriefing, they sang the songs from the movie at the top of their voices until they pulled in the driveway.

Hope took her PJs into the bathroom to change. She hoped Sydney wouldn't notice or say anything if she did. Hope didn't think she could undress in front of anyone ever again, even Sydney. When she walked back into the room, Sydney stood in her PJs yawning.

"Looks like I'm not the only one who's beat, huh?" Hope was thrilled that Sydney was tired. Maybe they wouldn't stay up late talking.

"Have you met any new people in your neighborhood?" Sydney flopped across the bed.

"Not really. I spend all of my time at the library. I did meet a girl our age there. Her name is Nikki. I haven't really gotten to know her. She's kind of quiet and likes to wear black and neon colors. I thought I saw her at the movies tonight."

"Why would she have been there when it is nowhere near your side of town?"

"Weird, I know, but it looked like her. I'll ask her about it the next time I see her."

"Something seems different about you, Hope. It's like you've gotten quieter since you moved."

"It's not like I have a lot of people to talk with during the day. Besides, you're supposed to be quiet in the library." She wiggled her eyebrows, causing Sydney to giggle. "I guess I've just gotten into the habit. There's no particular reason." *Well that sounded convincing, even if it is a stretch.*

"I guess that makes sense." Sydney yawned again.

Hope waited for the next question, but it never came. Sydney was fast asleep with the light on. Hope didn't mind. She pushed Sydney over to one side of the bed and threw the covers over her. She switched off the light and climbed into bed with her best friend.

On the way home in the morning, Hope felt normal in the back seat of Mrs. Clarkston's car, with Sydney. Maybe she could get through this after all. As they turned onto her new street, she saw a blue pickup truck in the driveway. Her heart beat so loud, Sydney and her mother had to hear it. Troy was talking to her mom on the front porch. Hope wanted to run, but she couldn't. Doing anything out of the ordinary might put her mom in danger.

Sydney tapped her on the shoulder. "Hello, did you hear me?"

"Did you say something?" Hope picked up her things, holding tight so Sydney wouldn't notice her hands trembling. "Sorry, I must have zoned out. I'm not sure why Troy's here, though." Hope's voice cracked.

"Who's Troy?"

"Just one of the movers." Hope's voice was unfamiliar to her.

"He's probably just checking with your mom to make sure everything was satisfactory. It's good customer service." Mrs. Clarkston turned off the car.

The familiar, acidic churning started up in Hope's stomach. A rank-tasting belch wiggled up through her mouth.

"Are you okay? You look green."

"All of a sudden, I don't feel great." Hope gave Sydney a weak hug. "See you later?"

"Yeah. Text me later if you want. Feel better."

"Will do."

Hope climbed out as Troy started backing his truck down the driveway. He made eye contact with Hope and winked; she stumbled and tripped over the curb as she rounded the car.

"Are you okay?" Mrs. Clarkston made her way to Hope. Hope got up without acknowledging Mrs. Clarkston's question.

"Mom?" Hope practically ran across the lawn. "What was he doing here?"

"Oh, he just wanted to make sure I was pleased with the job and he dropped off some flyers. They finally agreed on a name and they're trying to get the word out." She looked at Hope. "What's wrong, honey? You look pale. Did you hurt yourself when you fell?"

"It's nothing." Hope tried to calm herself by taking a deep breath and releasing it slowly. Was Troy trying to catch her alone again? She had to focus on something else or she was going to scream.

"Thanks for bringing Hope home for me." Hope's mom waved.

"You're welcome," Mrs. Clarkston called as she started the car.

Hope didn't stay on the porch and wave with her mom. She went straight to the bathroom and lost the Chick-fil-A she'd eaten for breakfast.

At this rate, Hope would never be able to forget.

CHAPTER 8

It was Tuesday afternoon before Hope saw Nikki at the library. She came out of the restroom just as Nikki finished her transaction with her "friend" Blake.

"Hey, Nik. What's up?"

"Not much. You?"

"Did I see you at the theater Friday night?"

"Oh, yeah. You saw me?" Nikki giggled a bit and picked up a book and began flipping pages.

"I thought so, but I couldn't figure out why you would be at that theater when there is one right around the corner from here showing the same movie." Hope looked directly at Nikki. She wouldn't drop the issue.

"What are you, a detective?" Nikki turned to face her head-on, the hostility was palatable. "I could ask you the same question." Nikki locked eyes with Hope, refusing to look away.

"Well, I was there because I was spending the night with a friend who lives near there. I used to live on that side of town."

"What?"

"Long story." Hope reached back to the cart to retrieve another book. "The Cliffs Notes version is my dad split, the money went with him, so we had to move."

Hope went back to shelving books. Nikki's face softened, and she pushed the cart down the aisle as they talked.

"That stinks. I totally get how parents can screw things up. Home sucks sometimes. I wish my dad would split, but he's set on making my life miserable." Hope stopped shelving books.

"He and mom fight all the time and when I heard you telling that lady," Nikki gestured toward Ms. Joyce, "that you were going to have some fun at the movies, I decided to take MARTA out there."

"Didn't your parents freak out that you went all the way across town on the subway alone at night?"

"They don't even know I exist except when they need someone to blame for something. I have to escape one way or another."

"What do you mean?" Hope returned the empty cart and retrieved another one full of books to shelve. Nikki stayed right behind her.

"You know how home can be the last place you want to be?" Hope knew all too well. "If I can't leave before the fighting starts," Nikki explained, "I'm trapped. I can't take it. It's been like this since my dad lost his job four years ago. So I learned another way to check out."

"How?" Maybe this would help her when Troy tried to invade her mind.

"I smoke a little weed. You can't get addicted to it and it's cheap. It's just enough to take the edge off so I can fall asleep. Besides, everybody at school does it."

Hope had never in her life considered drugs. This was crazy. Why wasn't she running away, and fast? Nikki's story was a little too familiar.

"Let me know if you ever want to try it. I've usually got some with me. No pressure."

"Thanks, but I'm good."

"Suit yourself." Nikki raised an eyebrow at Hope. "I'm outta here. I'll see you in a few days."

"In a few days? Why in a few days?"

"Because"—Nikki patted the bag in her pocket—"that's about how long it lasts before I have to buy more."

"You mean you come to the library to buy drugs?" Hope was shocked, but tried not to let her mouth hang open. She didn't want to draw attention.

"Yeah," Nikki laughed at the expression on Hope's face. "You don't think Blake comes to the library to read, do you?" She turned and walked to the door. "Later!"

Hope always thought of drug users as losers who couldn't complete sentences, but she liked Nikki. She could relate to Nikki's crappy home life. Her problem was the home itself. It felt like prison. It mocked her and reminded her how used and filthy she was. Even so, she wasn't desperate enough to smoke pot—not yet, anyway.

A couple hours later, when Hope and her mom got home, the voice on the answering machine stopped Hope dead in her tracks.

"Hey, Ms. Ellis, this is Troy. I just wanted to call and say thank you for the referral. We're scheduled to help the Marshalls move next week. I'll be dropping by with a thank-you gift for you and Hope. If you're still at work, I'll just leave it with Hope. Thanks again for getting the word out about our company."

The answering machine beeped again and played a message from Hope's new school about registration. Hope barely made it to the bathroom before she threw up.

Why was Troy tormenting her? She didn't know if he would ever leave her alone. Every time she heard his voice, it was like he violated her all over again. This could not go on. She had to escape.

Escape. Isn't that what Nikki said weed helped her with?

* * *

Friday afternoon, Nikki showed up in the library again. Hope had her hands full with Little Tots Day Care's library day, but she needed to talk with Nikki. She looked over her shoulder; Ms. Joyce's attention focused on a line of kids stacked up to check out books. Coast clear.

Hope signaled to Ms. Joyce that she was going to use the restroom, but she went to Nikki's usual spot and cornered her instead.

"Okay, I'm in." Hope tried to sound calm.

"What are you in for?" Nikki smirked as she turned a page in *The Scarlet Letter,* Hope noticed the title in gold leaf on the binding and wondered if Nikki had any clue what she held in her hands.

"I want to try weed. Will it cost me anything?"

"Nah!" Nikki put the book down. "You can try some of mine. If you like it, I'll introduce you to Blake and he can hook you up. Just make sure Ms. Joyce doesn't see you talking to him."

"Okay, so when do we do it?" Hope was eager now. She was desperate to escape the nightmare.

"Well, I know you're here all day today. You don't want to come here high until you know how you'll respond to it. Once you get used to it, you'll be able to cover yourself. I can walk into my house high as a kite and my parents are clueless. What are you doing tomorrow?"

"My mom planned a yard sale. She wants to get rid of a bunch of stuff, including a mountain of my books. It's like she never gets tired of changing things around on me." Hope was startled to realize that she blamed her mom partially for what happened. "Why don't you come by and I'll introduce you to her. She's been saying I need to make some new friends. Maybe she'll let me leave the yard sale and go hang out with you."

"Okay, write your address down and I'll be there, but not early." Nikki held out her hand and a pen.

What was she doing making plans to meet Nikki to get high? Had she lost her mind? She never thought she'd resort to drugs, but she never thought she'd be raped either.

CHAPTER 9

Saturday morning started way too early for Hope. She would've preferred to be sleeping, but promised to help with the yard sale. In return, her mom promised her a cut of the money they earned.

Hope was shocked at how early people came out for a yard sale. When she raised the garage door at seven in the morning, people were waiting. The ad in the paper was a good idea. From seven until around ten a steady flow of people made their way through the garage. Hope went in the house three times to drop some of the cash so they wouldn't have so much outside with them. They were really doing well. It was approaching noon and the garage was half empty. Nikki walked up just as Hope finished up with a young girl who bought several of her books.

"Hey!"

"Hey, yourself. What time did you guys get out here?" Nikki looked around at the people rummaging through boxes.

"We opened the door at seven, but there were people parked along the street waiting for us. It was crazy. Come meet my mom." Hope grabbed Nikki's arm and dragged her to the table that was full of knickknacks and old lamps where her mom haggled with one of the elderly neighbors. "Mom, this is my friend Nikki, from the library."

"Hey, Nikki, it's nice to meet you. What are you up to today?"

"I'm headed to the park and wanted to see if Hope could come too, but I forgot about the yard sale."

"Go ahead. You've worked hard all morning. I can handle the rest of this. We've only got another hour or so."

"Are you sure, Mom?" Her mom would die if she knew what she was up to. Instead of encouraging her to go with Nikki, she'd lock Hope in the house and call the cops.

"I'm sure, honey. Have fun. Just take your cell phone with you and be home in time for dinner."

"Thanks, Mom, you're the best!" Hope gave her mom a hug before she left. "I'll help you clean everything up when I get back."

"Nice to meet you, Ms. Ellis."

"Nice to meet you too, Nikki."

"Your mom seems cool. What gives?"

"I don't want to talk about it." Hope looked down at the ground.

"Hey, don't worry about it. Whatever it is, a little weed will knock the edge off and make your troubles fade away, even if it's only for a little while."

"How long does it last?"

"Depends on how much you smoke and how often. A couple of hours most of the time. Long enough for me to go to sleep without getting raked into my parents' drama."

"So where are we going?"

"There's an old abandoned house back in the woods near the park. You can't see it from the road. No one ever goes near it anymore. It's my hiding place when I need to escape."

The house was all gray, the brambles that used to be the hedges were gray, the siding that used to be white was gray, even the gray concrete seemed too gray. The windows that weren't boarded over were cracked, and only about two of the shutters were still attached. A few others littered the perimeter. Hope found it to be eerily exciting and depressing at the same time.

"How'd you find this place?"

"Back when my parents first started fighting, I went out for a walk. They were so pissed at each other, they didn't even notice me leave. I must've been ten. I was wandering around when I saw the path that leads back here. I just followed it." They went around back to sit on the steps.

"You ever go inside?"

"I have. If it's raining. But it smells nasty in there. I'd rather sit out here."

"Good idea. It looks like it might fall down any second."

Nikki pulled out a bag of weed and started rolling a joint. As Hope watched, she started to question herself. Did she really want to do this?

Nikki paused to look at her. "You don't have to do this."

"No . . . no, I really do. Go ahead."

"Me first." Nikki smiled as she lit the joint. She sucked in a few times and blew the smoke out away from Hope. It smelled strong and damp, a cross between fresh mulch and burning pine. "Ahh, that's good stuff."

Nikki's eyelids drooped a bit as she held the joint out to Hope. "Take it and inhale, but not too much."

"How?"

"You do it like you're taking a breath."

Hope's hands trembled as she took the joint. What could it hurt? It was just once, right? If she didn't like it, she didn't ever have to do it again. Besides, Nikki was being so nice about it, even though she was asking a lot of questions. She couldn't back out now. She'd look like a pansy. She put the joint to her lips and took a drag. Her throat burned and she coughed, hard.

"Not so much at first." Nikki laughed at her. "You've got to get used to it."

Hope eventually got the hang of it. Nikki let her take a couple of extra drags, to make up for the first one, she said. They passed it back and forth.

The pot kicked in quickly, and Hope and Nikki rolled on the ground laughing. Hope felt heavy and slow, but happy, like she didn't have a care in the world.

"See, I told you this would help take the edge off of your worries."

"What worries?" Hope giggled.

"You have an ant on your face."

"Really?" Hope fell into hysterics. An ant on her face? That was the funniest thing she ever heard. When she was done laughing, Nikki looked at her with her head cocked to one side and said, "Seriously, Hope. What's your deal?"

The dam broke. She didn't mean to tell her, but she couldn't stop once she started. It was like the high fueled her confession. Nikki didn't seem shocked. In fact, when Hope was done talking, Nikki reached out and touched her cheek. Her eyes were sad and Hope felt closer to her in that moment than she'd felt to anyone since it happened.

"Ant's back," Nikki told her, and brushed the tender touch across Hope's cheek like she was flicking an ant.

"You're funny." Hope doubled over in hissing laughter.

Finally, Hope had someone she could be real with and not have to worry about her reaction. On the walk home a few hours later, they'd look at each once in a while and erupt in laughter.

"Thanks, Nik. You really helped me today."

"That's what friends do, right? We are friends, aren't we?"

"You bet." Hope threw her arm around Nikki. She wasn't sure who needed whom more.

Nikki walked Hope to the door.

"Take a shower and change clothes so your mom doesn't smell smoke on you. Trust me, I learned the hard way. I'll see you next week at the library."

"Yeah . . . definitely."

As Hope climbed out of the shower, her mom yelled that pizza had arrived. She was starving. She didn't remember being so hungry in a long time.

"One piece or two?" Her mom turned to her as she walked into the kitchen.

"Definitely two, maybe even three. I'm starving! I don't know if it is from the yard sale or the park, but I could eat a horse."

"What did you girls do this afternoon?"

Hope paused. Had she said something she shouldn't? Did her mom suspect anything or was she just asking? "Oh, you know, just walked around and talked mainly."

"Nikki seems like a nice girl. I'm glad you're finally making some friends. It will make the start of school easier. Now, you want some great news?"

"What? Are we going to Disney World before school starts?"

"I wish. But we did make $756 at the yard sale."

"Wow!" Hope said with a mouth full of pizza. "That's a lot of money."

"It is, and since a lot of what we sold belonged to you, I thought I should give you a bigger cut than I originally planned. You worked hard and were willing to help out on a Saturday, so I am going to give you $256. I'll use the rest to buy what you need for school. If we have any left I'll put it in savings."

"Really?" Hope screamed. "You're giving me $256? I can't believe it." Hope jumped up and hugged her mother.

"Honey, you earned it. You worked really hard and you never complained. I'm proud of you. Now what are you going to do with your money?"

The first thing she thought of was weed, but she couldn't very well tell her mom that. "I don't know. I think I'll save it for something special."

"Very wise, Hope. Yet another reason to be proud of you."

Hope felt a knot in her stomach. If her mom really knew what Hope was thinking, she wouldn't be proud of her. She was a whore, a liar, and now a druggie. What would be next? Suddenly she couldn't swallow her pizza.

*　　*　　*

Sunday morning, Hope wanted to stay home, but she wanted to see Sydney too, sort of.

Sydney ran to her the minute she got out of the car.

"I can't believe school starts in less than ten days. I hardly saw you at all this summer. Soon it'll almost be impossible for us to hang out," Sydney whined.

"We'll have breaks." Hope tried to sound positive, even though it was getting harder and harder to be around Sydney. Her life was normal. She was a normal girl with parents who were married and who loved her. She was pure. She told the truth. She was everything Hope used to be.

"Yeah, assuming we don't get loaded down with projects and stuff."

"It won't be so bad. We'll just have to stay caught up so we can see each other on weekends."

"You're right." Sydney hugged Hope hard. A rogue tear slipped out of her right eye. "Now let's get to Sunday school. You've missed the past few."

Chapter 10

Hope shelved her last cart of books when Nikki walked in.

"Hey, girl!"

"Hey, Nik. What's up?"

"You get a break anytime soon?" Nikki looked over at Ms. Joyce.

"Ms. Joyce, I'm going to take my lunch break outside today, okay?" Hope stuck her head in the office and grabbed her lunch bag.

"That's fine." Ms. Joyce didn't even look up from the computer.

Hope walked outside with Nikki. When she got to the picnic table, she offered Nikki half of her sandwich.

"No thanks, I slept in and just ate breakfast. Blake called me and wanted me to come by and see if you were ready to make your own purchase."

Hope looked up from her sandwich. Nikki looked straight at her.

"There's no pressure, you know. You might not be ready for it. I just plan on meeting him here tomorrow, and he wanted to know how much to bring with him. That's all."

"I can't keep sleeping on the sofa when school starts. Mom's gonna insist I sleep in a real bed. If I have to stay in that room for more than five minutes, I'm going to have to be high. Even then, I think I'll sleep on the floor."

"Hey, it's okay." Nikki put her hand on Hope's. "That guy is a jerk. What he did to you was wrong. You wouldn't be normal if you could just sweep it under the rug."

"Thanks."

"I'll tell Blake to bring a little extra. Start out small and work your way up. Just do a twenty bag. That should last you a while."

"Okay."

"I better get out of here so you don't get in trouble." Nikki stood up to leave. "I'll be back by here tomorrow. When should we come?"

"Come around five thirty. I'm usually shelving books, and Ms. Joyce is in the office finishing up on the computer. She won't even know you're here."

"Later!" Nikki crossed the street and started down the sidewalk toward the MARTA station.

Hope walked back into the library and started shelving books, trying not to think of the line she was about to cross.

Hope's mom arrived right at six as she promised.

"Hey, honey, how was your day?"

"Pretty good, yours?"

"Crazy busy! We picked up some new accounts, and I'm going to have to work a little later for the next few weeks. I might need you to stop the weekday work and just hang out at the house."

Hope could taste the vomit in her throat. She couldn't quit now. She had plans to meet Blake tomorrow and wouldn't stay in the house alone all day. She had to think of something.

"What if I just take MARTA home?" Hope swallowed hard, forcing the bile back down. "Nikki takes it down here a lot. I'm sure she'd meet me so I don't have to ride alone. Would you mind? I really don't want to leave Ms. Joyce hanging. Plus, volunteering looks really good on college applications." Hope knew her mom was already trying to figure out how to send her to college, even if she wasn't taking her on visits yet.

"Well, I guess if Nikki rode with you, I'd be okay with it. But text me the minute you get home so I don't worry. I'll probably have to work until eight or so the rest of this week and next. I hate doing it the last week of summer and your first week of school, but everyone else agreed to do it. I can't afford to be the only one in the office clocking out at five while everyone else stays. I need this job."

"I'll be fine. I'm in high school now."

"Okay, Miss High School, I'll leave some money on the kitchen counter tomorrow and you can order pizza for dinner."

Everything is working out. Nikki might even hang out with me until Mom comes home so I don't have to be home alone. At least that would keep her out of her parents' way. How pathetic am I? Will I ever be able to be alone again?

*   *   *

Nikki and Blake showed up a little after five thirty, but what did she expect from druggies? Hope saved the shelving in the back corner so Ms. Joyce couldn't see her when they got there. Nikki walked up but Blake lingered back a couple of stacks.

"Hey, you got your money?"

Hope looked around the corner and saw the office door closed. "Yeah." She pulled it out of her pocket and held it out to Nikki.

"You hang onto it. I'll send Blake over here. You're a big girl. You can buy your own weed."

Hope's heart started racing. *What do I say? Should I make small talk? Should I call him by name or play dumb?* About that time, Blake walked over to her.

"I decided I don't want this book, but I'm not sure where it goes. Can you put it back for me?" He handed her the book with a small baggie of weed on top.

"Sure." Hope's voice cracked. She picked up another book with the hand she had the money in. "Try this one and see if you like it better." She spoke louder than necessary. She passed the book and money to him, hoping he wouldn't notice her hand trembling. He took the twenty and handed her the book back.

"No thanks, I'll wait till next time to check something out." With that he turned and walked out of the library. Hope turned toward the cart and stuffed the bag deep into her pocket. When she turned back around, Nikki was standing there.

Hope startled. "Geez, you scared me half to death."

"Calm down, girl. You look like you're about to pass out. Breathe. You did fine. I'll be waiting for you outside when you get off work." And she was gone.

Hope went through the library collecting books that were left on tables or in the computer carrels. Ms. Joyce came out of the office just as Hope made her way back to the front desk.

"Everyone left early tonight. We don't have to throw anyone out this time." Ms. Joyce laughed at her own joke.

"Nope, just you and me." Hope grabbed her things. "I'll see you in the morning."

"Is your mom here?"

"No, I'm taking MARTA home. Mom has to work late today."

"I'll be happy to run you home, if you'd like. Just let me lock up."

"It's okay." Hope tried to sound grateful. "My friend Nikki is waiting on me outside. Thanks for the offer. See you later."

"You too, Hope. Be careful."

"Yes, ma'am."

"Finally!" Nikki stood leaning against a tree as Hope walked out. Blake stood beside her but he was busy texting someone.

"Hope, meet Blake, officially. Blake, Hope."

"Hey!" He tossed his hair out of his eyes.

"Hey, yourself." She tried to sound calmer than she felt.

"I invited Blake to head to the house in the woods with us. Since you don't have to rush home, I thought we'd hang out a while. Are you up for that?"

Hope wasn't sure what Nikki was up to, but she wasn't going to act like a baby in front of Blake. He was going into tenth grade, and way too cute. She'd go.

"Sure, I'm game."

"Let's split, ladies." Blake threw an arm around each of them. At first Hope was very tense and a bit uncomfortable but she soon realized Blake didn't mean anything. He was just a big flirt. They made their way to MARTA, laughing and telling stories all the way to their stop. They didn't have a long walk to get to Hope's house.

"Let me throw my stuff inside so I don't have to haul it around."

Nikki and Blake waited at the end of the driveway while Hope opened the garage door and threw her stuff inside. They were laughing when she walked up.

"What?" Hope felt like she'd missed out on a joke.

"Oh, nothing. Blake here just thinks you're cute."

"Shut up, Nik." Blake grinned at Hope, then turned back to Nikki, "So where's this hideout you've been talking about?"

"A girl's gotta keep some secrets, right, Hope?" Nikki glared at her.

Hope couldn't move. What was up with Nikki? Was she about to tell Blake her secret? Surely she wouldn't. They were friends. Hope was so lost in her train of thought, she didn't realize Nikki and Blake were walking away.

"Ya coming?" Nikki called over her shoulder.

"Yeah, yeah! I'm coming. Who are you? My mother?"

As soon as they arrived at the house, Blake pulled a thick joint out of his pocket. "Ladies, my treat." He winked at Hope. Nikki took the joint and lit it like they smoked together every afternoon. She passed it to Hope.

"Oh, yeah! This is good stuff." As if she could tell a difference between good stuff and bad stuff. It didn't take long for Hope to feel stress free. She didn't mind when Blake sat down and threw his arm over her shoulder. All was right in Hope's world. Her mom wouldn't be home for a couple of hours, the pot worked its wonders, and a really cute guy seemed attracted to her. This was a good day in her book.

Blake's phone vibrated and he turned to her with a sleepy smile. "Duty calls, ladies. I gotta bounce." He stood up and made his way through the woods without looking back.

"He's so cute," Hope said, a little louder than she intended.

"Yeah?" Nikki jabbed Hope. "I didn't invite him to hang out with us so you could steal him away from me. Thanks a lot." She stood up and started to walk off.

"Nik, wait up!" Hope ran to catch up with her. "I didn't try to steal anyone. All I did was sit down. He came over to me. I didn't know you were dating him. Sorry."

Nikki turned around, "I'm not, but it doesn't mean I don't want to." She punched Hope playfully in the arm.

"Well, you coulda told me."

Nikki just shrugged and started walking toward Hope's house. Hope loved hanging out with Nikki. She never stayed mad about anything and she was the opposite of judgmental.

"Hey, what do you have to eat at your house? I'm starved!"

They walked out of the woods toward her house. "I've got money for pizza. What do you like on yours?"

Thirty minutes later, the Domino's truck pulled into the driveway. Within minutes the girls downed two pizzas and an order of breadsticks.

"My mom is going to kill me. We ate everything." She licked the sauce off her fingers.

"I'm outta here. The last thing I want to do is hang around while someone else's parent goes off. I get enough of that at home. See you tomorrow." Before Hope could question her, Nikki disappeared.

Her mom would be home in about an hour. She cleaned up the pizza mess and got out of her clothes. They smelled. Suddenly, panic hit her in the face. She was alone. What if Troy came over? He could be out there right now just waiting for Nikki to leave.

Hope pulled the bag out of her pocket. A little more wouldn't hurt. The only way she could stay alone was high. Wasn't that why she bought the pot to begin with?

She rolled a joint the way Nikki had showed her and went out the back door. She tucked herself in between the big trash and recycling cans so nobody could see her if they caught a whiff, and thought about how nice it felt to have Blake sitting beside her earlier. But as cute as Blake was, it wasn't worth ruining a friendship over.

She took a couple of drags, and when she felt herself relaxing, she put the joint out, then stuck it in her baggie for later. The phone rang as she walked in the door. She jumped a foot in the air.

"Hello." She was speaking a little slower than normal.

"Hope, is that you?" Her mom's voice shocked her back into reality.

"Oh, hey, Mom."

"You don't call or text me when you get home like we discussed, and all I get is a 'Hey, Mom?'"

"Sorry! Nikki came over, we ordered pizza, got to talking, and I totally forgot to text you. I really am sorry. Are you on your way home?"

"Yeah, but I need to get gas on the way, and I didn't want you to worry about me. Obviously, I'm the only one worrying."

"Come on, Mom, I really am sorry. I didn't mean to worry you. Nikki and I just lost track of time. Please don't be mad."

"Oh, forget it! I'm too tired to be mad. Did you and Nikki leave me any pizza?"

"Oops!" Hope giggled. She had to watch it or her mom would know something was off with her. "We were starving. We ate it all. Do you want me to order another one?"

"Never mind." Hope heard her mom's sigh. "I'll just pick something up on my way home. I'll be home soon."

"Okay, be safe."

Hope snuggled in on the sofa with a book. She really wanted to lay back and enjoy the euphoria, but she couldn't afford to slip up in front of her mom. Her mother trusted her and Hope didn't want to do anything to damage that trust.

"Hope? I'm home." Her mom walked in the door and collapsed into the chair beside her. "You're doing laundry?"

"It's the least I could do after Nikki and I ate all the pizza. I know you had a long day at work and wouldn't have time to get to it." Hope felt like she had covered her tracks and won brownie points with her mom all at the same time. Maybe she could handle this new habit after all.

CHAPTER 11

"Good luck on the first day, Honey."

Hope hugged her mom good-bye and glanced at her watch.

"Have a good day at work."

There was a knock on the door before Hope made her way back to the kitchen.

"Nikki? Is that you?"

"Who else?" Nikki called out.

Shaking her head, Hope opened the door for Nikki, who seemed to be awfully cheerful for so early in the morning.

"You ready for your big day?" Nikki nudged her as she passed by on her way into the kitchen.

"What do you mean?" Hope followed behind her.

"We could get high before school if you're nervous and you think it will help."

"Is that your answer for everything?"

"Hey, don't harp on me. I just thought it might help you out, that's all. Forget I said anything. Have you got any food? I need to eat."

"What's new? Here, have a muffin." Hope slid the plate of muffins her mom had made toward Nikki. "Did you smoke up on your way over?"

"What makes you think that?" Nikki stuffed a second muffin in her mouth.

"Oh, I don't know, the fact that you're about to start your third muffin before I eat one. You always eat like an animal when you're high."

"There you go, harping again. If I didn't know any better, I'd think your name was Harper instead of Hope." Nikki smiled with her mouth full, which made her look like a chipmunk.

"Come on, we're going to miss the bus if we don't go."

"Yes, Mother." Nikki grabbed one more muffin as they headed toward the door.

*   *   *

Nikki wasn't in any of Hope's classes, but they did have the same lunch period so they met in the cafeteria.

"How are your classes?" Hope set her tray down beside Nikki.

"They're classes. What do you expect? I'm not a bookworm like you. I'm just here because I have to be. I did, however, notice a lot of cute boys."

"Why am I not surprised? You know, I could help you with your schoolwork if you want."

"No thanks. I'm good."

Nikki came home with Hope after school and they raided the refrigerator. Hope picked up her phone to text her mom.

Home.

Thanks for letting me know. There are cookies I made in the pantry. I'll see you at 8.

K.

"We have cookies." Hope turned around to find Nikki already in the pantry looking for something else to eat.

"Are you high again?"

"Maybe . . . you need to catch up." Nikki started giggling uncontrollably.

"I'm good. I want to get my homework done before my mom gets home."

"Whatever, I just thought you might want to go with me and Blake to the house. He said he would be there around five."

Hope was torn. She wanted to get her homework done. She'd always made it her practice to do her homework as soon as she was home from school. She hated it hanging over her head. Just then, the phone rang.

"Hello."

"Hey, Hope," Sydney said, "How was your first day of school?" Sydney was the only teenager Hope knew who would talk on the phone as much as she texted. When Hope hung up, Nikki had already taken off to meet Blake. *Just as well.* Hope wanted to get a good start to her school year. She grabbed her books and crashed in front of the television to work on her homework. She had been working hard for about an hour when the doorbell rang.

Was Nikki back? Maybe she and Blake were just messing with her. She looked out the window and saw Troy's blue pickup truck backing out of the driveway. Her heart began to race. Her legs buckled beneath her, so she leaned up against the door. Would this never end? Why did he insist on popping up? Once she was sure he was gone, she opened the door. There was a basket of flowers on the front porch with a note attached that read, "Thanks for the referral. Troy and James."

Just touching something he touched made her want to throw up. She wanted to throw the flowers away, but she remembered the message on the answering machine and knew her mother expected them. She put them on the counter, shaking. How could she stay in this house? Every time she got comfortable and started to feel secure, Troy would show up or leave a message. There was only one way to cope with this.

Hope went to her room and pulled her bag out from under her mattress. With trembling hands she plucked out the joint from the other day. Only after she finished did she start to calm down. She had a hard time focusing. She decided to forget the homework and relax instead.

* * *

"Hope Louise Ellis, where are you? We need to talk."

Hope was just climbing out of the shower. "I'll be right there, Mom." She pulled on her clothes and brushed out her hair. Her clothes hung on her. She ate all the time. Still, she was losing weight.

She walked into the kitchen. "What's up?" She poured herself a glass of milk.

"This!" Her mom slapped a piece of paper on the counter. "What's going on, Hope? You're making Cs and Ds in all of your classes except literature and you're only carrying a B there. You didn't think I needed to know this? Where is my straight-A student? How in the world did this happen?"

"I'm sorry. I thought I could bring the grades up before you found out and then it wouldn't matter."

"What I don't understand—" her mom began to pace around the kitchen—"is how your grades ever got this bad. Hope, you're a great student. Every time I come home you're either on the sofa with a book or you're in the shower. What's going on?"

"Mom, stop yelling at me!" Hope raised her own voice. "You don't know what it's like to have to go to a school where you only have two friends. I'm an outsider. I don't know what I would do if it wasn't for Nikki and Blake."

"Blake? Who is Blake?"

"Just a guy in school, Mom, nothing more."

Her mother looked at her thoughtfully. "Something has to change, because this is unacceptable." She waved the progress report in the air. "If these grades don't come up soon, and I mean soon, you will face punishment. Do you understand me? No cell phone, no Nikki, nothing."

"Yes, ma'am, I understand."

CHAPTER 12

Bound and determined to bring up her grades, Hope decided to go to the library instead of hanging out with Nikki and Blake. She hadn't seen Ms. Joyce in a long time and she could avoid being home alone.

Hope made her way to the MARTA station without any trouble, even with an armful of books. She tripped as she stepped onto the train, dropping her schoolbooks everywhere. "That was graceful," she said to no one in particular as the doors closed.

"Here, let me help you."

Hope locked eyes with the guy as he started collecting her books. She thought, *Maybe there are still some nice guys in the world.*

"Thanks. I normally do a better job of walking."

"No problem." He handed her the books. "The name's Sweet T, but my friends just call me T."

"Sweet T? That's unusual. Anyway, thanks for the help, T. My name's Hope."

"Pretty name for a pretty girl." He took his seat. "You always read that many books?"

Hope looked down, hoping she wouldn't blush from the comment.

"No, I'm trying to bring my grades up."

She sat down across from him with her books in her lap. She tried to get a look at him without being obvious. His arms were solid and well defined; he looked like he worked out a lot. He had a square jawline with a very thin beard. He looked like he could be a rapper or something, but he didn't seem rough. How many guys on MARTA would get up to help a girl with her books? Hope decided he must be kind. At the next stop he got up to leave, but not without giving her a flirtatious smile. "Later, Hope."

"Later," she said trying to sound more grown-up than she was.

Hope practically floated to the library. She couldn't stop thinking about Sweet T. It wasn't like she'd ever see him again, anyway.

Ms. Joyce looked up from the front desk just as she walked in the door.

"Well, hello stranger. What brings you here?" Ms. Joyce came around the desk with a smile.

"My grades." Hope gave her a hug. "They aren't where they need to be and I need to get them back on track."

"Sounds like a good plan. Do you want a study room or do you want to work out here at a table? I can clean out some space in the office if you need more privacy."

"No, I'm good out here." Hope unpacked her books.

With a lot of catching up to do, Hope worked nonstop for over two hours, only occasionally slipping into a daydream about Sweet T. She looked up when she heard Ms. Joyce lock the library door.

"I'm sorry. I didn't realize it was so late! I'll be out of here in a minute." Hope shoved the sprawl of books and papers into her backpack.

"Why don't you let me give you a lift home? It's on my way and it will give us a chance to catch up."

"Thanks," Hope said, "I didn't really want to walk home from the MARTA station in the dark."

"Is everything okay, Hope? You seem a little troubled and you're looking awfully thin. You can talk to me, you know." Ms. Joyce watched the road as she rounded a long, slow bend.

"I'm fine, really." Hope wouldn't look Ms. Joyce in the eye. "I just let my grades slip and my mom is ready to ground me for life if I don't bring them back up. That's why I came by the library today to work on my homework. I need to focus on school instead of hanging out with friends. You'll be seeing a lot of me."

"Well, that will be just fine with me." Ms. Joyce reached over and squeezed Hope's hand. "I'll look forward to it."

She chatted easily with Ms. Joyce. It was good to talk to somebody who didn't know anything of the Hope from before the move.

"Thanks for the ride. I'll see you tomorrow."

Hope started toward the door. Was someone sitting in the dark on her front porch? She froze. Whoever it was moved. Hope jumped back and nearly threw her backpack.

"Geez, Nik, you scared me half to death! What's up?"

"Where've you been?"

"I went to the library to get my homework done. I've got to do something about my grades or my mom is going to kill me. How long have you been here?"

"Oh, I don't know, ever since Blake split. Apparently, he has a thing for you. He wasn't too interested in hanging out with me once he learned you weren't around." A tear rolled down her cheek. "No one wants to hang out with me, not even a pothead."

"That's not true, Nik. You could always come to the library with me after school."

"Not a chance. I think I'm allergic to homework."

"Even if there's a hot guy on MARTA?"

"Even then."

In the dim lighting of the porch light, Hope noticed the hurt in Nikki's eyes. "Are we good?"

"Yeah, we're good." Nikki stood up to leave. "I know you've gotta go in. Your mom has been home awhile. I'll see you tomorrow."

"Yeah, tomorrow."

A twist of the aromas of tomato, garlic, basil, onion, and melting cheese drew Hope into the kitchen.

"Hey, Mom. Is that lasagna I smell? And garlic bread?"

"You're late. Where have you been? I tried calling your cell phone and didn't get an answer. I was worried."

"Sorry, I turned it off in the library and I forgot to turn it back on." Hope pulled the crust off a piece of garlic bread and crammed it in her mouth.

"You went to the library today?"

"I have to do something to get my grades up before you kill me, so I've decided to take MARTA to the library every day after school and work on my homework."

"Why don't you just come home and do it?"

"There are too many distractions. With Nikki and Blake wanting me to hang out every day, I just need to go to the library. If I'm there, I won't be tempted to goof off."

"I don't like you riding MARTA after dark, Hope. You never know what kind of people hang out in those stations at night."

"I won't, Mom. I'll be home before dark. I just lost track of time tonight. Ms. Joyce dropped me off. I didn't really want to ride MARTA after dark, either, and neither did she. She said she'd give me a lift anytime, as long as she doesn't have to go anywhere." Hope crammed more bread in her mouth.

"Well, I'm proud of you. It sounds like my daughter is back. Now go wash your hands for dinner before you eat it all standing here." Her mom swatted her on the backside with the greasy spatula. "Go, so we can sit down at the table like civilized people."

"All right, all right! It smells terrific. I can't wait."

"Hurry up. I'm starving."

Hope savored every bite of her mom's lasagna and wiped her mouth. "You should open a restaurant, Mom. People would be lined up around the building."

"I'm glad you liked it; now go get on your homework."

"I'm finished with homework. I got it all done at the library. Why don't you go soak in a hot bath and I'll clean up the kitchen? You deserve some time off."

"Thanks, honey. I think I'll take you up on that." Her mom stood up to take her dishes to the counter.

"Leave it, Mom. I've got it." Hope shooed her out the door.

While her mom soaked in the tub, Hope turned on the radio and began cleaning the kitchen. She realized she'd missed spending time with her mom. She'd forgotten a lot of things since she met Nikki and Blake. Sydney left her countless messages and Hope hadn't returned any of them. After she turned on the dishwasher, she reached for the phone and dialed Sydney.

"Hello."

"Hey, Syd. What's up?" Hope tried to sound like they had talked every day.

"Hey, yourself. Where in the world have you been? I've left you a hundred messages!"

"I know. I'm sorry. I haven't been a very good friend. It's been harder than I thought adjusting to a new school. I don't know what I would do if it wasn't for Nikki."

"You've always got me."

Tears of regret snuck into Hope's voice, "Syd, you're the best."

"Yeah, I know. Don't cry, or I will too." They laughed. "Look, I gotta run. Dad just got home and we're heading out to dinner. I'll call you this weekend to see if we can hang out."

"I don't know if I can hang out with anyone for a while. My grades haven't been the best, and Mom is tightening the reins until I bring them up."

"No problem. We can just catch up on the phone until you get out of the doghouse. Take care."

"Yeah, you too. Tell your parents I said hello."

Hope grabbed the book she'd checked out of the library and flopped onto the sofa. She hadn't really relaxed in a long time.

CHAPTER 13

"I've got some good news," Hope announced as she walked into the library grinning from ear to ear. "I've brought all of my grades up to Bs. My teachers told me if I continue to work this hard, I could even have As before report cards come out in December." Hope was so proud, she couldn't stop smiling.

"I knew you could do it!" said Ms. Joyce. "I'm so proud of you. Your mom will be too. Now I have some news of my own. I've been asked to teach a class at the technical college this quarter. Starting next week I'll be teaching a seven o'clock class every Monday, Wednesday, and Friday."

"Wow! That's exciting for you!" Hope was genuinely happy for Ms. Joyce, but she couldn't hide her disappointment.

"I'm sorry I won't be able to drive you home those nights."

"I understand." Hope didn't want to dampen Ms. Joyce's excitement. She smiled. "I'll just leave earlier on those days. Maybe I'll even get home in time to surprise my mom by cooking dinner for her for a change."

"This doesn't start until next week, so I can still take you home tonight. What have you got planned for the weekend?"

"Schoolwork." Hope rolled her eyes. "I have a huge project for science class. I'll be working on it all weekend. Teachers don't think we have anything better to do on the weekends."

"When is it due? Let me help you pull some books."

"Not until next Friday. I want to get a head start."

"That's my girl."

It was a good thing Ms. Joyce drove Hope home that night—between her backpack and all the books she checked out, she had a heavy load.

"What in the world have you got there?" Her mom grabbed some books out from under Hope's arm as she staggered through the door.

"I have a huge science project due next Friday. I thought I'd work on it this weekend." She dumped the remainder of the books on the table.

"I brought home a lot of work to do too. I'll order some takeout for dinner and we can both get started. Would you rather have Chinese or pizza?"

"I don't care, I'm not very hungry."

"Are you feeling okay? You haven't been eating much lately. You and Nikki used to eat me out of house and home, and now you are hardly eating enough to survive."

"I'm fine. I've just been too focused on my grades to eat."

"You're starting to sound like your old self again. I think I'll order pizza."

* * *

"Hey, Ms. J," Hope called as she walked in the door Monday afternoon. "Are you nervous about teaching your first class?"

"A little; I spent all weekend preparing."

"You'll do great!" Hope placed an apple on Ms. Joyce's desk.

Ms. Joyce smiled, "Thanks, Teacher's Pet."

Hope went to work collecting the books she needed for her project. She wanted to make sure she had them all before she sat down. She couldn't afford to stay late. At five o'clock she packed her things for home.

"Hope, how in the world are you going to get home with all of those books? Do you want me to drop some of them off on my way home from class tonight?"

"Are you kidding? This is only six! Remember last week? I had to make two trips between your car and my house." Hope stacked her books. "I can cram half of them in my backpack and I'll carry the rest. Good luck tonight! You'll have to tell me all about it tomorrow."

"Thanks, Hope. I'll see you tomorrow."

Hope was looking at the index in one of her books as she stepped onto MARTA.

"What, no grand entrance this time?"

Hope looked up and saw T looking at her with a smile. What was it about the way this guy looked at her that made her heart go flip-flop? He had to be at least five years older than her but looked at her like he could only see her.

"Hey, I didn't see you there." She smiled at him, trying to sound calm.

"I guess not, with your nose in a book." He motioned to her so she sat beside him.

"You don't have as many books tonight. Not as much homework?"

"No, I have a project due this Friday, but I basically finished it tonight. I just need to cross-reference a few things." She held up the books. "I've got some more in my backpack."

"Very thorough; I like that in a person. What ya gonna do to celebrate?"

"I don't know yet, but my mom is going to be totally proud. My grades weren't great at the beginning of the year."

"I'm sure your parents are very proud of you."

"It's just me and my mom now. That is, when my mom isn't working overtime."

"Well, I'm sure she'll reward you for your work. If I had known you finished your project today, I would have suggested we grab ice cream or something."

"Oh, you're sweet." She smiled at him.

"That's my name, Sweet T. I gotta live up to it. Well, beautiful, this is my stop. I'll see you later." He waved as he stepped off the train.

Hope couldn't believe that guy. He was so nice, gorgeous, and he actually seemed interested in her. She didn't feel uncomfortable around him at all. In fact, she felt safe with him. It was nice to have someone take some interest in her, even if it was only on MARTA.

Hope walked home as fast as she could, thinking how grateful she was for Ms. Joyce's rides. Even six books were heavy after a couple of blocks.

Hope let herself in the house and looked at the clock. Her mom wouldn't be home for at least an hour. She set her books down, and her thoughts turned to Sweet T. The phone rang. She jumped. Why? Why was she so nervous just because the phone rang? It didn't have to be Troy. It's not like he was watching the house. Or was he?

She looked at the caller ID and recognized her mom's work number.

"Hey, Mom."

"Hey, honey. I was about to leave you a message to tell you I would be a little later than expected. When did you get home?"

"I just walked in the door. I made sure to leave right at five so I didn't have to walk home in the dark."

CHAPTER 14

"Thank you so much for dropping Hope off tonight, Ms. Joyce. You have been such a blessing to Hope, and really, to me too, especially with all the books she's been hauling back and forth for her project."

"Please, you can call me Joyce. Hope is the one who is a blessing. I enjoy her company. Have a good night you two, and good luck on your project tomorrow, Hope."

"Thanks, Ms. Joyce."

Hope and her mom stood on the porch until Ms. Joyce pulled out of sight.

"How was your day, sweetheart?"

"Okay, but I'm ready for this project to be over." Hope dumped her backpack on the floor.

"Let's plan on going out for dinner Friday night to celebrate. You can invite Nikki to join us if you want."

"Thanks, Mom. I'll need something to look forward to after all of this work."

Hope was exhausted. "I think I'm just going to veg in front of a movie for a while, Mom. I worked nonstop at the library."

"That's fine, honey. I'm going to warm up some dinner and then go to bed early."

Hope popped a DVD in the player and was asleep before the previews were finished.

***

Hope's mom drove her to school Friday morning so she could take in her project. She had her report, her PowerPoint, and a trifold board to display her findings.

Hope had science first period. She went straight to the classroom and started setting up for her presentation.

"Someone's here awfully early." Mrs. Sockwell looked up from her desk.

"I had my mom drive me to school so my trifold wouldn't get messed up on the bus. Is it okay if I set up since I go first?"

"You're fine, dear. We have about twenty minutes before the bell rings, so you can relax. I'll let you know when we're ready to start."

Mrs. Sockwell paused from writing the presentation order on the board. "Hope, I must say, I have been impressed by the change in attitude I've noticed in you these past few weeks. It's like you woke up from a bad dream or something and really started applying yourself. I'm looking forward to your presentation."

The day flew by after that, and Hope ran to the bus to tell Nikki the good news.

"I got a ninety-eight on my project. Can you believe it?" Hope bounced up and down on her toes. She was so excited, she couldn't be still.

"Yeah, I can. You've been working on that thing nonstop. Does this mean we can finally start hanging out again?"

"Sorry, Nik, but I was desperate to bring my grades up. This should get my mom off of my back for a while. Let's go celebrate!" Hope squealed.

Hope's mom wasn't home when they got there. Hope really didn't expect her to be, but she secretly hoped she might've left work early. They went to the kitchen for a snack. She picked a note up from the counter.

Hey, honey! I know today went well. I made you a peach pie. It's in the refrigerator. You and Nikki try to leave me a piece. I'll be home by six o'clock and we can start celebrating. Love, Mom.

"Nik, you're in for a real treat. My mom's peach pies are the best in all of Georgia. She keeps peaches in the freezer because she knows it's my favorite. She made one and left it in the refrigerator for us."

"What are we waiting for? You get the pie and I'll get the plates."

Hope cut each of them a huge piece of pie and warmed them up in the microwave.

"Got any vanilla ice cream?" Nikki poked her head in the freezer.

"Nope, but we have whipped cream."

"That'll do." Nikki pulled the spray can out of the refrigerator. "It's better with vanilla ice cream. Next time you do something great and we get to celebrate, tell your mom to get vanilla ice cream." Hope laughed.

They took their pie to the couch and surfed TV stations while stuffing their faces. When their pie was gone, they finished off the spray can of whipped cream, laughing all the while. When Nikki got up to go to the bathroom, Hope looked at the clock. It was already six thirty. *What's keeping mom?* The phone rang.

"Hope, honey, I have some bad news. The boss is making all of us stay tonight until this project is complete. I told him it was a big night for you. He told me I wasn't being a team player. I feel so bad, but I have no choice."

"Mom, I was so looking forward to this. Nikki and I have been waiting all day to go out and have some fun. I can't believe this. It's like that stupid job is more important to you than I am!"

"That's not true, Hope, and you know it. I'll make it up to you. I promise."

"Never mind! Just forget it." Hope slammed the phone down, sat on the floor, and started to cry.

"What's going on?" Nikki walked up behind her.

"Mom just canceled. Apparently, her boss snaps his fingers and she jumps, even if it means breaking plans with me." She wiped her eyes.

"Sorry, friend, no dinner out tonight. There will be no celebration of any kind. Just leftovers. Yippee!" Hope sat there like a deflated.

"Hey, we can have our own celebration." Nikki took Hope's hands and pulled her up off the floor. "I just happened to see Blake today, so I can host a party for us. You up for it? Sure you are. One joint and you'll be feeling better. How long before your mom gets home?"

"Who knows? Why?"

"I just didn't know if you wanted me to call Blake and have him grab a few friends and come join us."

"Better not. I'm just now getting out of the doghouse. I can't afford to have her coming in on a party."

"Okay, just the girls. Why don't you go warm up leftovers while I roll us a joint? We can take our party outside so we don't leave any evidence behind. We'll have a good time. Trust me."

"Thanks, Nik." Hope hugged her. "You're the best!"

"What are friends for?"

As Hope and Nikki finished the joint and went back inside, all thoughts of her mom's broken promises faded away.

* * *

"Hope Louise Ellis!" Hope heard her mom screaming. "What is that smell?"

Nikki jumped up from the couch with a jolt. "I gotta go!" She was gone before Hope could clear the fog out of her head. Nikki was a great friend, but she was quick to bail when trouble came.

"Mom?" Hope tried to rub the sleep out of her eyes. She and Nikki must have come in from smoking and crashed on the sofa. "When did you get home?"

"Apparently not soon enough! What have you been doing?"

"Just hanging out, Mom, not that you'd care. All you seem to care about these days is your stupid job." Hope started down the hallway.

"Don't you smart-mouth me! You get back here this instant, young lady!"

Hope made her way to her room, slammed the door, and locked it behind her. Her mom sure knew how to put a damper on a perfectly good high. Hope grabbed her pillow and stretched out on the floor. In minutes she would be sound asleep again.

Hope woke up with a horrible backache. Sleeping on the floor was not the smartest thing. It took her a few minutes to clear her head. As she did, she remembered the argument with her mom. That wouldn't be the end of it, and she knew it.

Her phone buzzed.

HEY!

It was Nikki.

Thanks 4 ur help last nite.

Sorry! Couldn't handle it. Get enuff of that at my own house. U grounded?

Idk. Haven't been out of my room yet.

K. Let me know.

There was no point in putting off the inevitable. Maybe she could convince her mom that the smell came from Nikki's jacket. She could blame it all on Nikki's older brother. Did Nikki have an older brother? Didn't matter. All that mattered was convincing her mom Nikki had an older brother.

Hope jumped in the shower and got dressed quickly. She found her mom in the kitchen sitting at the table staring out the window. She sat down. Her mom's eyes were red and puffy from crying.

"Mom, I'm sorry we fought last night. I didn't mean to yell at you. I was just so upset you dumped on me when we had made plans to have a celebration dinner."

"Dumped on you! Is that what you think I did? Honey, it is because of you that I'm killing myself to keep this job. I didn't want to stay and work late any more than you wanted me to, but I didn't have a choice. Somebody's got to put a roof over our heads and food on the table. We don't have any other options." Her mom wiped the tears streaming down her cheeks.

"Mom, please don't cry." Hope got up and put her arms around her mother.

"Sit down, Hope! We're not finished here. What did I smell when I came in the house?"

"Well, I was going to tell you last night before you starting accusing me and Nikki of doing who knows what. Nikki's brother is trouble. He came by here looking for her. When we went to the door to talk with him, he was smoking a funny looking cigarette. All I can figure is the smoke got in the house and on our clothes. That's all, Mom." Hope tried to sound convincing.

"Hope, I don't want any guys over at the house when I'm not here, and that includes Nikki's brother. You understand me?"

"You didn't care about the movers."

Hope's mom's eyes looked like slits of rage. She hadn't seen her mom so angry since right after Dad left.

"That's different and you know it." Her mom's voice was eerily quiet.

"Yes, ma'am." Hope suddenly felt deflated and all the anger seemed to pool at her feet. "I told Nikki your rule, but what was I supposed to do? It's her brother. He didn't come inside." The lies were too easy.

CHAPTER 15

Hope spotted T immediately when she stepped on MARTA Monday afternoon. He smiled at her. She couldn't help but move in his direction as he patted the empty space beside him.

"How is it you're always here when I take MARTA?"

"Just lucky, I guess." He winked flirtatiously. "What did your mom do to reward you for your science project?"

"Ha!" Hope laughed bitterly as she plopped into the seat beside him. "She let me down, that's what she did."

"Whatcha mean?"

"My mom's boss made everyone stay late on Friday after she promised she'd take me and my friend Nikki out. She said we'd have to do it another time. I know it wasn't her fault, but I was really disappointed and angry."

"But it was your special night. She could have gotten off work if it mattered to her." He shook his head. "That stinks. I wouldn't have ditched you like that. If it were me, I'd have told the boss to get over it 'cuz I had plans with my girl."

"Yeah, well, Mom stayed and worked, so Nikki and I threw a little impromptu celebration."

"Okay, okay, I like this friend, Nikki, and I don't even know her. What'd you guys do?"

Hope looked down at the ground, not sure if she should tell him how they spent their evening. "Just hung out, you know."

"Sounds to me like you don't want to gimme the details. All right, I see how it is. I thought we were friends and all, but you don't have to tell me if you don't want to." T looked away.

"You might think bad of me if I tell you what we did." Why was his opinion so important to her?

"Try me, girl. I'm certain anything you did would be all right by me." He reached over and squeezed her hand.

"She had a bag of weed and we threw ourselves a little party. We got high and just chilled out on the sofa." Hope looked up to see how he would respond.

"Hey, that's cool. You had to do something to celebrate. After all, you were looking forward to your mom being there for you and she wasn't. I tell you what, when will you be riding MARTA again?"

"Wednesday, why?"

"Why don't we meet and I'll take you out for ice cream for our own celebration. We can meet at your stop and walk down the street to the Dairy Queen, unless you'd rather celebrate another way?"

"I can meet you at five o'clock at the MARTA station if that works for you."

"Perfect!" He pulled her hand to his lips and kissed it. "It's a date." He stood up as the train came to a stop. "See you Wednesday, beautiful." He winked at her as he got off the train.

Hope's heart melted. She could hardly stand it. How did she get so lucky? She never felt fearful around him, only safe and protected. Maybe the fact that he was older than her provided a sense of security, or the way he immediately came to her defense when her mother hurt her. Either way, she felt like he wouldn't let anyone hurt her.

Wednesday morning, Hope tried on five outfits before settling on her skinny jeans, boots, and a black sweater. She wanted to look her best. She had a date with T, or at least she told herself it was a date. Isn't that what he had said as he stepped off MARTA?

* * *

"Hey, you! Are you deaf? I've been calling your name since the bell rang."

"Sorry, didn't hear you." Hope had been focused on T.

"No kidding! You want to hang out today?"

Hope's mind went into high gear gathering a plan. If she said she was going to the library to do homework Nikki would bug out quickly.

"Can't do it. I've got a huge test to study for so I'm headed to the library. Do you have anything you need to work on?"

"Are you kidding me? All I've got to work on is relaxing. I just spent seven hours in prison. No thanks! You can have it. Catch you later." Nikki made her way down the hall.

While Hope walked to the train, butterflies began their dance in her stomach. Why was she nervous? It's not like T really thought of this as a date. Who was she kidding? What would he see in her?

She stepped on MARTA and looked around, halfway expecting him to be on the train already, but he wasn't there. It wasn't time. She had an hour and a half before she was supposed to meet him. Why hadn't she suggested they meet earlier?

Ms. Joyce was busy on the phone when Hope walked in, so she got to work on her homework. She wanted to get it out of the way and enjoy her time with T. If she was going to use schoolwork as her excuse for being late for dinner she needed to make sure she got it all finished.

Hope finished her last math problem just in time to pack up and make it to the station. Ms. Joyce and Hope had both worked hard all evening. They didn't say more than hello to one another.

When she arrived at the MARTA station, T was waiting for her.

"Hey, sweetheart." He smiled as he checked her out from head to toe. "You ready to celebrate?"

"Absolutely!" Hope tried not to sound too eager, but she couldn't help it. She felt like Cinderella out with Prince Charming.

"Here." He reached for her backpack. "Let me carry that for you."

"Thanks." She smiled up at him nervously. She wasn't sure what to do with her hands now that he had her backpack. He reached over and took one of her hands and held it as they walked.

"You still up for ice cream?"

"Ice cream's good." What was wrong with her? Ice cream's good? She'd better get it together and act like she had a brain in her head or else he would only see her as a little girl.

The Dairy Queen was a short walk from the station. T insisted Hope get a banana split since she was the girl of honor. He didn't order anything for himself. He told her he would just have a bite or two of hers.

When she sat down in the booth, he tossed her backpack in the seat across from her then he slid in beside her.

"I ain't gonna sing or anything," he said, "but I did get you a little something to celebrate."

Hope turned to face him and found him extremely close. Her heart started racing and her stomach felt nervous.

Without breaking eye contact, T took her hand and placed a small box in it. "Congratulations, sweetheart!" He didn't let go of her hand.

Hope wasn't sure what to do. She didn't want to make a fool of herself so she smiled. "Thanks. Can I open it?"

"Yeah." He let go of her hand so she could lift the lid. What had T given her? She hadn't known him long and already he was giving her something in a jewelry box? He was too good to be true. She opened the box to find a silver necklace with the letter "T" dangling from it.

"This way you can always have me with you even when I'm not. It'll serve as a reminder you're my girl." He pulled it out and began to hook it around her neck.

"You want me to be your girl?" Hope nearly squealed.

"Only if you want to be." He looked shy, almost bashful as he waited for her response.

"Yes!" She looked into his eyes. *A girl could get lost in those eyes.*

As she ate her banana split, little giggles escaped her lips. She couldn't help it. T wanted her to be his girl. Hope hadn't felt wanted by a man since the day her daddy walked out. It felt good.

"This has been the best celebration ever."

"This is just the beginning. Now that you're mine, things are going to change. You gonna share that or eat it all yourself?"

Hope fed T a spoonful, but some of the whipped cream got on the side of his face. He licked it off without taking his eyes off of her.

"Don't want to waste anything."

Hope didn't want their time to end, but she knew she needed to go to avoid getting in trouble with her mom. She wished she could stay here all night with T.

T stood up, took her hand, and helped her slide out of the booth. "I know you've gotta go. I wish we could spend the whole night celebrating, but your mom will give you hell if you aren't home before dark, huh?"

"I know. I wish we could just hang out all day." She threw her trash away and walked outside as he held the door for her.

"Why don't we?"

"Why don't we what?"

"Why don't we spend a day together?" T stopped walking and turned her toward him. "We could pull it off. Next Wednesday. You go to school like normal, then at lunchtime you just ditch and meet me down here at the station. We'll hang out the rest of the day."

"I don't know, T. I'm not sure I can do it."

"What's wrong? Don't you want to spend the day together? I guess I thought there was more going on here. Thought you were my girl."

"I am your girl!" Hope reached over and took his hand, trying to reassure him. "I just have to figure out how to do it without getting caught."

"You leave that to me. I'm a pro at not getting caught. Do your teachers know you live alone with your mom?"

"I doubt it. They hardly know my name."

"Good." When they reached the MARTA station, he asked Hope for a piece of paper and a pen. He wrote a note that read: *Please excuse Hope from school after lunch. She has a doctor's appointment.*

"What's your last name?"

"Ellis."

He signed the note *Mr. Ellis* and handed it to her.

"All you gotta do is turn this in Wednesday morning. Then meet me here and your cute little butt is covered." He winked at her.

"You think of everything, T." She took the paper as their train pulled up.

They took a seat together. Hope's heart did a flip-flop. Just the thought of spending the day with him made her feel giddy.

"What time does your lunch period start?"

"I have second lunch, so I leave class at 11:42 to head to the cafeteria."

"Okay, then I'll meet you at the MARTA station next Wednesday and we'll spend the rest of the day together, just you and me. Wear something special because it's gonna be a special day."

T blew her a kiss as he stepped off MARTA. "See you Wednesday." The doors closed. Hope sat back in shock. She couldn't believe it. T not only wanted her to be his girl, but now he was making plans to spend the day with her. "Wear something special," he'd said. What on earth would she wear?

CHAPTER 16

Sunday night Hope searched through her entire closet trying to find something suitable to wear for her date with T on Wednesday. Everything made her look so young. She needed a plan.

"Mom?"

"Out here!" I'm trying to organize these boxes so I can find all of the holiday stuff." Hope followed her mom's voice to the garage. "Do you realize Thanksgiving is just three weeks away? Then it will be Christmas, and before you know it you'll be turning fifteen."

"Hey, Mom, slow down. No need to rush things." Her mother always got excited about the holidays. "I was wondering if we could go to the mall Monday after you get home from work since we didn't get to celebrate last week?"

"I think so. I could use a break."

Hope hugged her mom. "Thanks!"

Hope's attitude had been bad for a week, so she knew her mom was thankful for the change. Hope had been sulking around, hardly speaking.

Monday afternoon, Hope skipped into the library.

"Hey, Ms. Joyce, what's up?"

"I think I should ask you that question. What put you in such a good mood?"

"Oh, nothing much. My mom is taking me out shopping today after work as a reward for doing so well on my project."

"How well did you end up doing?"

"I made a ninety-eight!" Hope smiled. She was proud all her hard work paid off.

"That's wonderful, Hope! I'm not surprised. You worked hard. I've never seen a student pour so much effort into an assignment."

She turned and walked into her office and came back out with a twenty-dollar bill in her hand.

"Here, I want you to take this and buy yourself something fun from me tonight when you go to the mall."

"Ms. Joyce, that's not necessary."

"I know it isn't necessary, but I want to do it." She stuffed the twenty into Hope's pocket.

Hope gave Ms. Joyce an unexpected hug.

"Thanks, Ms. Joyce. You're a great friend!"

"I don't know about that, but I like you, and I think you deserve to be rewarded for doing well."

Hope could hardly concentrate on her homework because of her excitement. She had invited Nikki to go to the mall with them that evening, but Nikki wasn't ready to be around Hope's mom.

"Since you used my brother, which I don't even have by the way, as an excuse for the smell in the house, I think I'll sit this one out." Hope just laughed. Nikki had a flare for the dramatic.

* * *

Hope beamed as her mom pulled up in front of the library after work.

"You're not excited, are you?"

"Really, Mom? Is it that obvious?" Her mom smiled.

"What do you think you'd like to get? A new CD? Or is there a movie out you'd like?"

"I was actually thinking of a new top or something, if you don't mind. Maybe even one of those sweater dresses everyone is wearing. I already have boots." Hope didn't want to ask for too much, but she really wanted to look nice on Wednesday.

"You know, I didn't really buy you any back-to-school clothes this year, so I think a sweater or a sweater dress would be okay. I still have some money we made from the yard sale, so let's do it."

Hope and her mom enjoyed being together, milling through the stores and trying on dresses at every turn. Hope pushed toward the trendy designs all the older girls wore, while her mom kept bringing things back to the conservative side. Finally, Hope crossed her fingers and emerged from the dressing room wearing a sweet, ruby-red sweater dress.

"Oh, Hope! That color looks beautiful on you. And the black belt will be perfect with your boots." Hope's heart leaped. *Score!*

"Now, how about some Chinese?"

"Sure!" Hope squeezed her mom's waist with one arm as they headed for the food court. "We haven't done this in forever." Hope and her mom used to shop together every month. But everything changed when her dad left.

"I know, sweetheart. I wish we could do it more often."

"I'm just happy we could do it tonight. Thanks for the dress. I think I want to wear it this week."

"That's a great idea!"

"Hey, I was wondering, do you think I might be able to start wearing eye shadow now that I'm in high school? All of the girls do, and I don't want to feel like a baby."

"You have beautiful skin. People wear makeup to try and look as beautiful as you do naturally. I've told you mascara and lip gloss are enough."

"Not even eye shadow?" Hope whined a little. She knew it would help her look a little older to wear more makeup. "I promise I won't wear anything tacky. I just want a little color."

"I think we're going to wait." This was her mom's way of politely saying no to whatever Hope asked.

Wednesday morning, Hope spent more time than usual getting ready. She used the straightener on her hair twice to make sure it was perfect. She even put on some of her mom's perfume. Grabbing her "T" necklace, she dropped it in her purse to put on at school. She didn't want to have to explain it to her mom. She also looked in the side zipper pocket of her backpack to make sure her excuse note was safe and secure.

"Hope, you're going to be late. Come on. Get out here so you will have time to eat breakfast."

Hope walked into the kitchen in her new dress and black boots. She also had on some dangling black earrings she'd bought with the money Ms. Joyce gave her.

"Wow! You look sixteen years old in that outfit."

"Really?" Hope seemed a little more excited than she intended.

"Hope, don't be in such a hurry to grow up. It happens all too quickly. You look beautiful. Are you sure there isn't some young man you're trying to impress?"

"Mom, please, can't I just enjoy looking pretty?"

"You certainly can, and you do look pretty. Now eat your breakfast and get that pretty little self of yours out the door so you don't miss the bus."

Hope grabbed her backpack and started for the door.

"Have a great day, honey. I'll see you tonight." Her mom fumbled with her car keys trying to juggle her briefcase and coffee mug.

"Bye, Mom." Hope kissed her mom on the cheek. "I love you!"

"Love you more!" her mom called out as she climbed in the car for work.

As Hope approached the bus stop, Nikki's chin hit the ground. "Shut up! Where did you get that dress? I love it!"

"Thanks. Mom got it for me at the mall. Are you sure it looks good?" Hope suddenly felt insecure.

"You're rockin' it, girl. I don't know how the boys are going to pay attention in class. You better not let Blake catch you in that or he'll follow you around all day like a lost puppy dog."

Hope could hardly focus on her teacher because she kept looking at the clock on the wall.

"Miss Ellis, do you have a date or something?" Mrs. Sockwell asked in front of the whole class.

Panic rose up in Hope's chest. Why did Mrs. Sockwell ask that question? Was she doing something wrong? Did she question the note Hope gave her about an early dismissal? Hope tried to act natural when she turned it in, but she knew her hands shook.

"Ma'am?"

"You seem to be more interested in the clock than my lecture," Mrs. Sockwell lifted an eyebrow.

"Oh, sorry, Mrs. Sockwell." Hope's cheeks turned pink. "I'll pay more attention."

Hope managed to get through the rest of her morning without drawing any more unnecessary attention. Everyone complimented her on her dress and told her how pretty she looked. She felt good about her date with T. Now all she had to do was get out of the school parking lot without anyone noticing her walking instead of climbing in a car with a parent.

*   *   *

"Damn girl, you look hot!" T reached for her hands. "You know how to mess a man up with that outfit."

Hope suddenly felt more confident. "You like it?"

"Like it?" He looked her up and down. "I love it! All you need now is some long nails and fishnet stockings and you would stop traffic."

Hope looked at him and smiled. "So, what are we doing today?"

"I don't know, but I can't keep you on the street long or else I'm gonna have to fight off the men like a pack of wolves." He lifted her hands and began inspecting them. "How about I take you to a salon I've heard about and get you some beautiful long nails? You can choose the color or get them done with that white stuff on the top."

"You mean French tips?" She and Sydney had done that for their eighth grade dance.

"Yeah, whatever it's called, let's do that. You look too hot not to have beautiful nails too. Nothing but the best for my girl." He put his arm around her waist, drawing her close.

Hope couldn't believe she was supposed to be sitting in ninth grade lit class and instead she was sitting in a chair at a nail salon having her nails done. T was the best.

Afterward, he took her to a quiet little restaurant she'd never seen before. He ordered a steak and told her to get anything she wanted. She felt like a queen.

"What are you thinking about, beautiful?" He looked across the table at her.

"I was just thinking how much fun I'm having and how I don't want it to end."

T slid out from his seat and came around the booth to slide in beside her. He took her chin in his hand and turned her to face him. Her heart raced. How had she gotten so lucky?

"It's not going to end, sweetheart; it's just beginning." He kissed her lightly on the cheek and then on the neck. Then he slid his plate across the table and finished his meal sitting beside her.

Hope's heart hammered in her chest. She had never had a boyfriend or been kissed except by that animal Troy. She had seen lots of movies and dreamed of what it might be like to be romanced.

"Hey, I have an idea." His voice pulled her out of her fog. "Some friends of mine are having a party tonight. Why don't you go with me?"

"I don't know if I can, T." She knew there was no way her mom would let her go to a party when she didn't know the people having it. Her mom would die if she knew she was with T right now.

"Why you want to hurt me like that? I thought we was having us a special day and now you ready to end it."

"It's not that, T." She reached over to take his hand. "My mom will kill me if I'm not home when she gets off work."

"Come on, baby. We're just getting things started. You can't leave. We'll figure something out. I wanted everyone at the party to meet my girl. I've been telling them about you, and they think I'm making you up. They said you're too good to be true."

"You've been telling your friends about me?"

"Of course I've been telling them about you. I told them how you took my breath away the moment you stepped onto MARTA."

"You mean the moment I fell flat on my face on MARTA?"

He smiled at her and held her eyes for a moment before speaking. "You weren't the only one who fell that day, sweetheart."

He stared at her lips. Hope tried to swallow the lump in her throat. She knew he was about to kiss her, not on the cheek or the neck, but really kiss her. She didn't know what to do. Before she knew it, his lips were on hers. He was so gentle, not forceful like Troy. He parted his lips and slid his tongue out and used it to part her lips. He began exploring her mouth with his tongue, sending her heart into overdrive. She didn't want to appear as young as she was, so she slipped her tongue into his mouth and tried to do the same thing he was doing inside of her mouth. She felt like she was just starting to get the hang of it when T ended the kiss.

"You can't tell me you're not staying with me after a kiss like that."

"Was it okay?" She suddenly became shy.

"It was all right, girl. Don't worry, I can teach you what you don't know. We just might have to practice a lot."

"I'm okay with that." She looked up at him and smiled.

"Okay, so it's settled. You're going with me to the party, and we'll figure out what to do about your mom later." He dropped a hundred dollar bill on the table to pay the check.

By the time they finished eating and made their way to MARTA, it was getting dark. The train looked deserted. Hope began to question her decision.

As the train went into the tunnel, T pinned her up against the seat, claiming her mouth with urgency and taking her breath away. He kissed her with a hunger that caused her head to spin. He dug his hands into her hair and only pulled back long enough to gain some air before kissing her again. She trembled. He left her speechless.

"I'm sorry. I couldn't help myself. You're just so amazing. I can't believe you're mine. I can't wait for my friends to meet you tonight."

Taking a deep breath, Hope smiled at him. She wouldn't allow a few butterflies to spoil her special night with T.

CHAPTER 17

The train ride was long, and Hope didn't recognize any of the stops. She started to get worried. When they reached their stop, T led Hope out of the station. She tried not to let her mouth gape open. Several buildings stood, run-down and boarded up, with windows busted everywhere. The grass was overgrown in the few places grass appeared to be growing. She had never been to this part of Atlanta.

"Where are we?" She tried to find anything familiar to latch onto to ease the nervousness crawling up her back.

"We're almost to the party. Listen, my friends don't know how young you are. I'm cool with it, but some of them might not be, so don't tell them how old you are, okay? If anyone asks you, just tell them you're eighteen."

She liked that T wanted her to be his girl even if she was a little younger than him. "Okay." She smiled, desperate to make him happy.

"In fact," he paused, "I've got a little something to help you out."

"What do you mean?" Hope fully expected T to pull her into his arms and kiss her as he had done on the MARTA.

He stopped walking and turned to her.

"Well, you already told me you and your friend do weed sometimes, so I figured you'd be willing to try something else, for me. Here." He placed a small pill in her hand. "Take this."

"What is it?" Hope was uneasy about the little pill in the palm of her hand. She wrestled with the desire to make T happy and her uncertainty about taking the pill. She had trouble swallowing pills and had never swallowed more than an aspirin before.

"It's just a little feel-good pill that will take the edge off of your nerves. I can tell you're nervous." He ran his hand up and down her arm, trying to wipe away her uneasiness. "This will help you."

"I don't know, T, I've never done anything but weed." She tried to sound older than she felt at that moment.

"Come on, baby, do it for me?" He kissed her on the cheek and down her neck. "I don't want any of my friends giving me a hard time about dating a younger girl, and I don't want them giving you a hard time about your age. If you do this, it will take care of everything. If it will make you feel better, I'll take one too."

He lifted her chin and looked into her eyes again. "You trust me, baby, don't you?"

"Of course I trust you." She nodded obediently and swallowed the pill.

T drew her into a hug and held her tight. "Now you're really mine."

They entered the house through the back door without knocking. The only home she walked into without knocking, other than her own, was Sydney's. Maybe this was T's home.

"Do you live here?"

"No, baby, but we family." He reached back, taking Hope's hand, drawing her close to him. He led her through a kitchen into a living room.

The room was dimly lit by a cracked lighting fixture that hung half attached to the ceiling. The furniture was ratty and faded, although no one seemed to care. Three guys were sitting around drinking beer and laughing. It all seemed harmless. So why did she suddenly feel alarmed and want to turn around and walk out? Where would she go? She didn't even know where she was. She couldn't embarrass T. These were his friends and he wanted her to meet them.

Hope noticed a lone girl in the group, dancing with a guy to a song she could barely hear, while the others watched. The dancing stopped when Hope and T entered the room. She tried to pull herself together and act natural when she noticed all eyes were on her.

"Hey, my man, T. What up?" One of the guys slapped T's hand with a handshake.

"Hey, bro, this here's my girl, Hope. The one I've been telling you guys about. Hope, this is Slick Rick. We go way back. That's JoJo, Tight Mike, and Big is dancing with Destiny."

"Hi." Hope cleared her throat. "It's nice to meet you."

"You want something to drink?" Rick held his beer out to her.

"No, thank you, I'm fine."

"Yes, ma'am, you are." He winked, undressing her with his eyes. It made her skin crawl. She moved closer to T. He slid a protective arm around her and took a seat on the sofa, pulling her down beside him.

Hope just listened as T and his friends talked. She didn't really know how to be part of the conversation. She held his hand tight as if holding on to a life preserver. Destiny didn't seem to have any interest in getting to know her. In fact, Destiny and Big seemed lost in their own little world on the dance floor.

"T, I don't feel so well. Can you take me home?" Hope whispered in his ear so his friends wouldn't hear.

"Oh, baby, it's just because you haven't eaten since you took that little happy pill. Let's go in the kitchen and I'll get something to eat. You'll feel better soon."

He pulled her up from the sofa. Hope's head spun. She walked beside T, but she couldn't feel her legs move. She didn't feel in control of anything.

"Here, baby." T handed her a plate of chips and salsa. She devoured it.

"I'm so hungry, I could eat a horse. More, please." A giggle escaped her mouth as she held out the empty plate for a refill.

"Feelin' better, girl?" T laughed at her.

"Yeah, I think I was just a little nervous about meeting your friends and all. I just need to relax," she said, a little more confident.

"Here." He handed her a cup with red punch in it.

"What's this?"

"Just a little fruit drink. He tapped his cup to hers. "Bottoms up." He drank the contents of his cup in one sip. Hope, wanting to fit in and make T glad he brought her, did the same. Within minutes she was giddy and light-headed. They made their way back into the other room. Destiny and Big were still dancing.

"Can we dance?" She slurred the words.

"Sure, baby, anything you want." T took her hand and led her to the center of the room. He pulled her tight up against him and started swaying back and forth in a seductive way. The others watched their every move, but suddenly Hope didn't care. She only had eyes for T. His friends seemed to like her, and she would learn to like them if it meant spending time with T. This was better than sitting at home alone waiting for her mom to get home from work.

The song changed and Hope noticed Destiny dirty dancing up against Big. The guys in the room started cheering. T looked at her and raised an eyebrow as if to say, "Are you up for it?" Hope felt bold. She wasn't about to be called out for being the baby of the bunch. She and Sydney had watched every dance movie that ever came out. She had never danced like that, but she thought she could pull it off. Before she knew it, T started grinding his waist against hers. She threw all caution to the wind, put her arms around his neck and followed his lead. What could happen? It wasn't like the two of them were alone. Hope tossed her head back and swayed to the music.

When the song finished, T gave her a long, hot kiss. She felt it all the way down to her toes. She enjoyed it, but she didn't want to do it in front of everyone. Embarrassment rose up in her as they cheered, calling out, "Get you some, T!" She wanted to pull away, but she couldn't. It was as if she had no control of her body. T controlled everything. She felt a vibration at her hip. T broke off the kiss.

"Baby, I've got to take this call. Why don't you dance with Rick?" T stepped out of the room.

Rick? Not Rick. He looked at her like a starving dog looks at a piece of meat. Before she could protest, Rick came up beside her and slid his hands down her side to her waist and began moving with her.

"It's time I had me a little taste of this sugar."

Hope watched T walk through the kitchen and out the back door.

"Where are you going?" she called out.

Surely he wouldn't leave her here. She turned to tell Rick she was going outside with T but before she could get the words out, Rick slammed his mouth down on hers. He started kissing her hard as he ran his hands up and down her body, grabbing and squeezing as he went. Panic took over. This wasn't what she wanted. This wasn't romantic. Troy's face filled her mind. Oh, God. What had she done? Had she done something to make Rick think she was interested in him? She only wanted to dance with T. She wanted to scream for help, but Rick never seemed to come up for air. Her heart raced. *This isn't happening. This can't be happening. These are T's friends. They wouldn't do this to him, would they? T! Help! Where are you? Aren't these your friends? Why aren't you stopping them?*

Rick moved her down the hallway without slowing down. Everything inside of her wanted to run, but her limbs had gone limp. Fear gripped her as she realized she had no control. Cheers echoed in her ears as Rick threw her on the bed. T's "friends" had followed them down the hall to the bedroom and were egging Rick on as he straddled her.

"I'm gonna show you how the big boys play, girl. You have no idea." Rick pulled off her panties and threw them over his shoulder.

Oh no, not again. This can't be happening again. T, where are you? Help me. I don't want this. Help! The words lodged in her brain and she couldn't make them come out of her mouth.

"Go, Rick! She wants it. Look at the way she's moving around there. She's just beggin' you!" someone yelled.

What kind of people are you? Why are you doing this to me? I'm T's girlfriend. Why isn't he here stopping all this?

Rick looked down at her with a wicked smile. He covered her mouth and proceeded to have his way with her while everyone watched. They chanted for Rick like he was about to score the winning touchdown at a football game.

How can they stand back and watch this? Where is T? Why doesn't he come back? Where's Destiny? Why doesn't she help me?

As if the nightmare couldn't get worse, one by one each of the men climbed on top of her and had their fill. If she started to move or fight, the others would pin her down, as if this was normal behavior. When they were finished, they walked out of the room, leaving her on the bed naked, exposed, ruined. She heard them in the other room drinking and laughing, laughing about her.

"Did you see the look in her eyes?" She heard one of them say.

It was a game to them. Hope wanted to die.

How did she get here?

She was a good girl, a good student.

She wasn't a whore! No, she wanted to save herself for marriage. First Troy; now this. No one would want her. Used goods.

No one would ever want to be with her now.

CHAPTER 18

Amanda Ellis tried to calm her nerves as she dialed Hope's cell number again. Voice mail. Where could Hope be? It was six o'clock, and still no call. Hope forgot to call a time or two when Nikki came home with her, but not lately. Amanda wished she had Nikki's cell phone number. Hope's phone could just be turned off. She tried their home number again and got the answering machine. The knot in Amanda's stomach told her something was wrong.

Why hadn't she connected with her new neighbors? Then she could have called someone to check on Hope. Amanda drove faster than she'd ever driven home from work, frantic to find her girl.

As she pulled into the driveway, a chill overtook her. Pitch black. Not one light shone through the windows. Most nights when she drove up, it looked like Hope was having a party.

"Hope? Hope!" Amanda couldn't get the door unlocked quickly enough. She went through the house, into every single room, calling. The house was empty.

A sliver of relief ran through her when she noticed the message light on the phone was blinking. Dropping her purse on the floor, she ran to the machine. "Thank you, Jesus. Hope Ellis, when I find you, you are so grounded."

"You have one new message." The automated sound of the machine echoed through the otherwise silent house. Amanda tapped her finger.

"Be Hope. Please, Jesus, let it be Hope."

The robotic voice was cold, empty, like Amanda's chest. "This is a message to alert you that your student was absent today from one or more of his or her classes. Thank you."

Steadying herself by leaning into the counter, Amanda swallowed hard. Moments ticked away as the weight of this reality settled on her shoulders. Hope had missed classes? None of this made sense. Hope never ditched school.

Amanda's beating pulse proved she was still alive. She didn't even realize she'd put her hand on her chest. There had to be a rational explanation.

The phone rang, interrupting her worry. "Hope, where are you?"

"Ms. Ellis? This is Sydney. Is everything okay?"

Disappointed tears pricked at the back of her eyes. "Hi, Sydney."

"Hi. I was calling for Hope. She hasn't been returning my calls or texts. I thought maybe she got a new number and forgot to let me know."

Amanda took a deep breath. "You mean she hasn't returned your calls today?"

"No. Not today. She hasn't returned my phone calls in a couple of weeks. Is something wrong?"

"Something is wrong, Sydney. I have a really bad feeling that something is very wrong. Hope's phone goes straight to voice mail. And she wasn't here when I got home from work. There is a message on the answering machine that says she was absent from one or more of her classes today." The tears couldn't be stopped. Amanda's throat tightened. "Something has happened to her. I just feel it. I don't know what to do."

"Ms. Ellis, I'm going to get my mom and we'll come over."

"Thank you, Sydney. I could really use a friend right now."

Amanda paced the living room. Her thoughts blocked each other. She stood still in the kitchen, feeling lost, listening for clues.

She was rooted to the spot when Sydney and Hannah rang the bell. It had only been a half hour, but it seemed like a day. She had to force herself to remember that walking meant putting one foot in front of the other.

"Come in." Amanda held the front door open, sobbing. Hannah pulled her into a hug. "I don't know what to do. I don't know where to start."

"I don't know how you're standing up. I can't even imagine what you're going through."

Amanda sighed in relief. Hannah was always level-headed, she couldn't think of a better friend to be by her side.

"Sydney," Hannah instructed, "go to Hope's room and look for a note or something. Hope might have left a message for her mom somewhere. Amanda, let's go sit down at make a list of what we know, and then we'll go from there."

Amanda let Hannah lead her to the kitchen table. Hannah pulled a note pad and a pen from her purse.

"When was the last time you saw Hope?"

"This morning. She was all excited about wearing a new dress I bought her Monday night. I took her out to the mall shopping because she got an A on a huge presentation. She worked her butt off on that thing for weeks." Amanda's head started to throb. She rested it on her palm, then drew in a deep breath, trying to stop her choked blubbering. "It was like my girl was back, you know, from before the move. We haven't done anything like that in so long. She was bubbly all night, so happy. She came into the kitchen this morning modeling her new dress. She looked like she grew up overnight." Amanda smiled through her tears. "She's a good girl. We've had a few bumps since the move, but she's never done anything like this. Never!"

"Don't worry, Amanda. I'm sure there's an explanation. We'll find her. Now what about friends? Are there any friends at her new school she might be hanging out with?"

"Only Nikki, but they never hang out at Nikki's house. They always come here. I think Nikki has a difficult home life. Her older brother is into drugs, so the girls stay here."

"Do you have Nikki's cell phone number?"

"No, I don't. I never thought to get it because they're always here. I don't even know her last name. Oh, Hannah, what if something awful happened to her?" Sydney stepped into the room.

Hannah and Amanda looked at her expectantly, "Anything, sweetheart?"

"No, Mom. Nothing."

"Let's check with your neighbors. Maybe one of them saw Hope this afternoon."

"All I know to do is go door to door because I haven't really met any of them. I've been working so much I haven't had time."

"I'm on it," Sydney said. "I'm gonna take this picture with me since they may not know Hope by name." Sydney pulled a picture off of the refrigerator. "I have my phone with me, Mom. Call if Hope comes home before I get back."

"Okay, sweetheart. Be careful. We don't want to have to worry about you too."

"Always, Mom!" Sydney headed out the front door.

"I'm going to call our pastor. He can get the prayer chain going for us and for Hope."

"Okay. Could you use your cell? I don't want to tie up the landline in case Hope tries to call. We don't have call waiting."

"Sure."

Amanda's worries deepened with each tick of the clock. This wasn't like Hope. Something had to be wrong. What could she do? While Hannah talked with the pastor, Amanda decided to walk to the bus stop and back. Maybe something happened to Hope on the way to or from the bus stop. She might have dropped something or there might be some kind of clue. She couldn't just sit there or she was going to lose it. She slid a note to Hannah, grabbed a flashlight, and stepped outside. It was cold. Did Hope have her coat? *Oh God, please protect my baby girl.*

Amanda walked the short distance to the bus stop waving the flashlight. With each step her heart sank. She stood at the gathering place, not knowing what she expected to find . . . something, anything to reassure her that Hope was okay. It seemed she had vanished. When she walked back inside, Hannah was holding Sydney. It was obvious Sydney was holding it together for Amanda's benefit. Hannah turned to Amanda. "Did you find anything?"

"Nothing." Amanda wondered if she would run out of tears.

Sydney put her hand on Amanda's shoulder. "None of the neighbors saw Hope today, Ms. Ellis. I'm really sorry."

Hannah reached for her phone.

"I think it's time to call the police. For all we know, she's been missing since early this morning." Hannah called the police and asked them to send an officer over right away. Sydney sat down beside Amanda and put her arm around her.

"It's gonna be okay, Ms. Ellis." Sydney was not convincing. Something bad had happened to Hope.

It was close to eleven o'clock when the police car pulled into the driveway. Hannah went to the door to let the officers inside. Amanda sat at the table, holding a cup of cold coffee in her hands. Tears still streamed down her face, though she'd stopped sobbing. She'd been sitting like that for at least an hour.

"Ms. Ellis? I'm Officer White and this is Officer Carlson. If it's okay with you, I'd like to ask you some questions while Officer Carlson takes a look in your daughter's room for any clues as to her whereabouts."

"Sure." She wiped her eyes. "Whatever you need. Sydney, would you take the officer back to Hope's room?"

Amanda watched them walk down the hallway. It should have been Sydney and Hope, not Sydney and a police officer.

A few minutes later, Amanda glanced down the hallway in time to see Sydney take a step back before looking her way, with a confused expression on her face, holding her hands up, parallel with her chest, a posture of denial.

Amanda watched Detective Carlson walk down the hall toward them. He held a plastic baggie and what looked like Hope's journal.

"Ms. Ellis, is your daughter a drug user?"

Amanda looked at the officer then Sydney. "Heavens no, are you crazy? She is afraid of needles, she can't stand smoke, and she has a hard time swallowing Tylenol. Why on earth would you think she was a drug user?"

"This would seem to indicate otherwise." The officer held up the bag of marijuana for her to see.

"Where did you find that?" Amanda shook her head in disbelief. A wave of shock ran through her.

"It was stuffed between the mattress and the box springs in your daughter's bedroom."

"That's crazy. Hope is a good girl. She wouldn't use drugs. She makes good grades. She's a good girl." Amanda wrapped her arms around her own waist and dug her fingers into her lower back. She winced at the pain. She tried so hard to hold on to something, she hurt herself.

"Settle down, Ms. Ellis. This might not be hers. She might be stashing it for someone. Who does she hang out with at school?" Detective Carlson asked with his pen ready to take down names.

"Nikki, but I don't know her last name. They met at the library over the summer and became good friends. Hope was volunteering at the library and came home one day talking about a girl named Nikki."

Amanda paced in front of the detective seated at her table.

"Nikki practically lived here all summer. In fact, she usually walks to our bus stop so she and Hope can ride to school together. Hope's never been to Nikki's house, at least not that I'm aware of. I think Nikki comes from a troubled home."

"Is there anything you can think of that would help us find Nikki?"

"She's in Hope's grade and she has a brother who is a drug user. Maybe Nikki brought that over to hide it from him or something. It's the only thing that makes sense to me."

"I also found her journal. Do you mind if I take it with us to see if we can find any clues about where she might be?"

"Officer Carlson, if it will help you find my daughter, you can take the whole house."

"There's not much we can do tonight, but we'll be at the school first thing in the morning to see which classes she attended yesterday, if any. We'll also talk with the bus driver and see if we can find this girl, Nikki, see if she knows anything. Do you have a current picture you can give us?"

Sydney handed him the picture she had taken from the refrigerator earlier.

"Thanks. We'll send out an Amber Alert and run this picture. Give us a call if she comes home. Sometimes kids cut class to blow off steam. We'll be in touch." He handed her his card.

"Thank you, officers."

"I'll show you out," Hannah said. When she returned, she looked at Sydney. "I'm going to call your dad to come pick you up. Like it or not, you've got school tomorrow. I'm going to stay with Amanda so she doesn't have to wait this out alone."

"Hannah, you don't have to do that. You have your own family to worry about."

"Nonsense, Amanda. You'd do the same for me."

Sydney threw her arms in the air. "Uh, hello? Why do the two of you get to wait for Hope and I have to go home? She's my best friend!"

"Because we're adults, and you're the high school student who has class tomorrow." Hannah drew Sydney into her arms. "Look, I know you're worried about Hope too, but it isn't going to do her any good for you to miss school or to be falling asleep in class."

Ed Clarkston arrived with an overnight bag for Hannah, and a hug for Sydney.

"Come on, young lady. Let the police do their jobs."

"Fine." Sydney blew out a long breath.

"Thanks, for letting Hannah stay with me tonight," Amanda said.

"No problem. I sent out an e-mail asking our friends to pray. Is there anything else I can do?" Ed ran his hands through his hair. "Is there anywhere I can go to look for her?"

"Yeah, Dad! Let's drive around the neighborhood! I'm never going to be able to sleep."

"You'll be fine, Syd. I'll make you some warm milk when we get home. C'mon, let's go." Sydney made a face. Ed kissed Hannah on the forehead. He held Sydney's hand to walk out to the car.

"I don't have any idea where she could be. Hope has been a homebody since we moved here. Other than school and the library, she's been home. Maybe her journal . . ." Amanda was frantic.

As Amanda slid the deadbolt in place behind Ed and Sydney, the fear intensified. *Where are you, baby girl?*

CHAPTER 19

Hope woke with a bright light shining in her face. It took her a moment to realize it was sunlight coming in from a window. Her head hurt. Her whole body throbbed with pain. Where was she? Where was T? Remembering the horror of the night before, she curled up in a ball and began to cry.

"Cryin' ain't gonna change things, girl."

Hope jumped at the sound of a stranger's voice. At least it was a female voice. Hope didn't think she could stand to look at another man, ever. She pulled the sheet tightly over her naked body. She squinted, waiting for her eyes to adjust in the light. Destiny stood in the doorway.

"It's time to get up, girl. We got a big day ahead of us."

"Where's T? Why didn't he come back? Why didn't he take me home last night?"

"Girl, you're lucky T didn't throw you out on your ass after what you did."

"What do you mean, what *I* did? I was raped last night by all of his friends and no one seemed to care, even you. I didn't want it. I didn't ask for it. They were like animals!" Hope screamed. She began to cry again.

"That's not the way T sees it. He said he walked outside to take a call and you went wild partying with his friends. He thought you were a good girl, special. He thought you were different, but now he says you'll just have to join the others." Destiny rolled her eyes in disgust.

"He came back? Why didn't he do something? I screamed for help and no one seemed to hear me. They just kept on as if I wasn't there."

"Oh, you were there, girl. You were there taking 'em on one right after the other. T walked in and saw you spread out on that bed, shook his head, and took off."

"Where are my clothes? I've got to get out of here. I need to get home. My mom will be worried sick." Hope dragged the sheet with her as she searched the room for her clothes.

"You don't get it, do you? You dissed T in front of his friends, his family, and now you think you're just going to walk out on him? That's not how things are done around here. He owns your ass now. You do what he says, when he says it; and right now he told me to get you cleaned up, fed, and give you something to wear."

"What do you mean something to wear? Where are my clothes? And nobody owns me!" Hope shook all over, but she couldn't decide if it was from anger or fear. "I was his girlfriend. But if he is breaking up with me, I'll just take my things and go." She wanted to sound confident but her trembling legs gave her away.

"Girl, you ain't goin nowhere! Besides, who would want you now? You're just used goods. You're bound to be an embarrassment to your mama just like you are to T. You tarnished his rep. You owe him and until he says you go, your skinny, little, white ass stays put."

Destiny wedged herself in front of the door. "Here." She threw a pair of jeans and a T-shirt at Hope. "Put these on and come to the kitchen if you want to eat. If you ain't there in ten minutes, I'll feed it to the dog."

Hope put on the clothes. They fit, but apparently Destiny didn't believe in underwear. Hope looked all through the room for hers, but she couldn't find them. There was no furniture in the room, other than a bed and a nightstand. She looked in the closet, hoping to find something there, but it was empty.

Hope pulled back the sheet that took the place of a curtain and saw there were bars on the window. She had to get out of there, but it wouldn't be through the bedroom. It was obvious Destiny wasn't going to step aside and let her walk out on her own. Her stomach growled, and she remembered Destiny's promise to feed her breakfast to the dog if she didn't come quickly. She didn't remember seeing a dog, but she didn't remember a whole lot before *it*. Hope walked barefoot into the kitchen, across a threadbare carpet that felt like sandpaper. Some of the wallpaper hung in peeling chunks. It looked like a grandma's house, except for all the empty beer bottles and full ashtrays. The stove and sink were avocado green. A small table in the center of the room held a bowl and a box of generic Cheerios. Four mismatched chairs sat around it. Destiny pulled milk from the fridge and put it on the table.

"You want coffee?"

"No, thank you. Where is T? When will I get to see him?"

"Soon enough. For now, he left me to teach you the house rules, teach you what's expected of you, and get you cleaned up."

"You make it sound like I'm a prisoner or something. I appreciate your willingness to let me stay here, but I really need to get home."

Destiny shook her head. "Listen here, ho, I'm not your girlfriend, your hostess, or your babysitter. You ain't in Kansas anymore, Dorothy. You ain't gonna click your heels together three times and be back home. Welcome to hell. I'm the guard. T is the warden. You'll leave when he says and not one moment before."

Her voice grew louder with each sentence, causing Hope's head to pound.

Destiny continued. "Don't piss me off with all this whining about going home. Don't make me deal with you. If you get out of line and start causing problems, it's my ass, so do what I tell you and you'll make it. You hear?"

For the first time, Hope took a good look at Destiny. She looked like she was pretty once. Now she looked old. Hope guessed she was about twenty, but the lines around her mouth, bags under her eyes, and the wan quality of her skin made her look much older. Tattoos covered her right arm. One of them simply read, "Sweet." She was so thin. How would this girl take care of her when she didn't look like she took care of herself?

Tears fell. Where was her mom? Would she be looking for her? Did she know Hope was being held against her will? Probably not. If she found out about the note from the attendance office yesterday, she probably assumed Hope cut school and was off having a good time with friends. What friends? *Oh God, how did I end up here?*

"Where is everyone?"

"Ain't nobody here but me and you right now. Don't worry, other people will be here later. Right now we have work to do. Wash your bowl and then come into your room. Everyone pulls their own weight around here. We ain't got no maid." Destiny poured herself a cup of coffee and left the room.

"Where's the dog?" Hope asked Destiny's back.

Destiny's laugh was brittle, "Ain't no dog here, not unless you count us."

Hope looked out the window over the sink, hoping someone would see her. But no one was around. The window had bars, just like the bedroom window. Despair began to soak into Hope's heart. Getting out of here wasn't going to be easy. For now, she'd have to do what Destiny told her and hope that T would come back soon so she could talk with him.

When Hope entered the room she had slept in, Destiny stood behind a chair, holding a pair of scissors.

"We need to do something about your hair. Sit down."

"I just need to wash it." Hope ran her hand through her hair.

"We'll wash it, but first we're going to cut it. Now sit down before I make you."

"I don't want my hair cut!"

"Girl, are you stupid? You just don't get it. You don't have options anymore. What you want doesn't matter."

For someone who looked so broken, Destiny was intimidating. Hope wondered if it was the anger that came out every time she spoke. Or the look in her eyes—the one that said, "I've got nothing to lose."

Hope sat obediently in the chair. Her bottom lip trembled as hair fell in her lap. Did Destiny even know how to cut hair?

"Not bad." She stepped back to look at it when she finished. "Now for the color. Have you always had brown hair?"

"Yeah." Hope wiped the tears from her cheeks. "My mom doesn't like colored hair. She said it looks fake."

"Well, Mama ain't around to stop me, so I'm coloring your hair. Let's go." Destiny pointed to the door with the scissors in her hand.

Hope walked back into the kitchen, reaching up to try and determine what her hair looked like. It had lots of layers. She hated layers.

"Bend your head over the sink." Destiny began rubbing the color in without saying another word.

"What color is it going to be?"

"I guess we'll see when I'm done."

Once the color was applied, Destiny made Hope sit at the table while she washed her hands. Her phone began to ring.

"Don't move." She lit a cigarette and walked out the back door with her phone.

CHAPTER 20

"I didn't wake you, did I?"

"No." Amanda yawned. "I can't believe I even fell asleep." Hannah and Amanda had paced and prayed all night long, running to the window every time they heard a car coming down the road.

"Sheer exhaustion took over, friend. You fought it until the sun came up." Hannah gave her a weak smile. "That chair couldn't have been comfortable. Are you ready for some coffee?"

"Sure." Amanda stared out the window over the sink, desperate for a glimpse of a girl in a red dress. Her eyes felt dry, and her head throbbed. "Did you get any sleep?"

"No. I think I had too much caffeine to go to sleep."

Amanda turned to her friend. "How many pots of coffee have you had?"

"This makes three or four, but who's counting?" Hannah reached up for a second mug to pour Amanda a cup. "Why don't you grab a shower while I make us some breakfast? The police officers are supposed to stop by this morning after they're done at the school."

Amanda hugged Hannah. "Thank you."

Ten minutes later, Amanda charged out of her room buttoning her shirt as she went.

"What is it?"

"I've got to get to the bus stop and see if Nikki is there. She might know something."

"Okay, but slow down. It's only seven o'clock. When does the bus come?" Hannah led Amanda to the table, forcing her to sit down. "Have some breakfast first."

"I can't eat anything."

"You have to. Write down your office phone number for me. I'll call your boss and tell him what's going on and that you won't be in today. Now eat."

Amanda pushed the egg from one side of the plate to the other. She finally took a noncommittal bite of toast, and though the misery never left her eyes, she managed to eat most of the egg and a piece of toast.

Hannah came in from the other room, continuing as if their conversation didn't lapse, "You may have moved out of our neighborhood, girl, but you never moved out of our hearts. We're like family and this is what family does for one another."

"Oh my gosh." Amanda dropped her fork. "I've got to call Charlie. He hasn't seen Hope in two years, but he's still her father. What do I tell him? I know he'll blame me for everything."

"Why don't you just wait until you know something? Besides, the police took down his name and address. I'm sure they'll contact him."

"I gave them his name and address? I don't remember what I said and what I only thought. I'm just so confused and scared and frustrated. Where could she be?"

"I don't know, but grab your coat and walk on down to the bus stop. I'll stay here, in case someone calls."

"Thanks, Hannah. You're really a lifesaver."

"Shh. Get going."

As Amanda turned the corner, she saw a police car at the bus stop. An officer she didn't recognize was talking with the students. Another officer had Nikki off to the side. She had to get to Nikki and see if she knew anything about Hope.

"There's her mom." Nikki pointed to Amanda as she walked up.

"Ms. Ellis, what's going on? Where is Hope?" Nikki cried. "I went to meet her at MARTA yesterday afternoon, but she wasn't there. I figured you picked her up, and now this officer is telling me she's missing." Nikki didn't bother to wipe her tears. Her cheeks were streaked with mascara. Amanda wondered if her mother knew she wore so much black eye makeup.

Amanda pulled Nikki into a hug. She gave the officer a questioning look.

"I'm Detective Johnson. Are you Ms. Ellis?"

"Yes, I am. Where are the officers who came to my house last night?"

"Ma'am, as soon as I'm done here, I'll come down to your house and explain everything and tell you what I know, okay?"

"Okay." She started to go but turned back to Nikki. "You haven't seen her anywhere?"

"Ma'am, I've already questioned this young lady and I promise to share everything with you as soon as I finish up with the bus driver, okay?" The officer was firm but polite.

"Detective, do you have a daughter?"

"Yes ma'am. I have three of them."

"Then you'll understand my need to talk with my daughter's friend right now." She turned back to Nikki. "Can I have your cell phone number?"

"Sure, Ms. Ellis." Nikki ripped paper from her purse and wrote it down.

"Thanks." Amanda turned to go home.

"Oh, and Nikki, what's your last name?" Amanda asked.

"Collins. Nikki Collins."

"Nikki Collins, thank you for your help. If you hear from Hope, will you let me know?"

"Yeah, sure." Nikki wiped her tears and tried for a smile. "Will you do the same?"

"Yes, and if you need to talk or just need a place to hang out, you're welcome to come by any time."

* * *

The detective seemed to be taking forever. The bus stop was less than a mile away. Why hadn't he come to fill her in? Hannah made more coffee, but Amanda was beyond coffee. She wanted answers and she wanted them now.

She called the front office at school. "Mrs. Sanderson, I'm calling about my daughter, Hope Ellis."

"Yes, ma'am. The police arrived a few minutes ago. They're meeting with the principal and the campus police officer. All I know for certain is that Hope didn't attend any of her classes after lunch yesterday. The police officer left the attendance office with a piece of paper in his hand, but I don't know what it said. Now, you didn't hear any of this from me, okay?"

"I understand. Thank you, Mrs. Sanderson."

"You're welcome. We're all praying for you and for Hope, Ms. Ellis."

"Thank you. We need all the prayers we can get."

Hannah finished unloading the dishwasher as Amanda hung up the phone. "What was all that about?"

"The police are at the school. Why would they go to the school after talking to the bus driver? The detective told me he would come here as soon as he finished."

"Maybe he got a lead he wanted to follow up on at the school before talking to you. That has to be good news, right?"

"The secretary said something about a note?"

The doorbell rang. They both jumped up and started toward the door. Amanda opened it to Detective Johnson.

"Ms. Ellis, I'm sorry to keep you waiting. May I come in?"

"Certainly. This is my friend, Hannah Clarkston. I'm sorry, but I don't remember your name."

"I'm Detective Johnson." He shook Hannah's hand.

"Would you like a cup of coffee?" Hannah asked the detective as she motioned for him to take a seat at the kitchen table.

"No, thank you, ma'am. I've already had my limit this morning. I would like to speak with Ms. Ellis for a moment, if you don't mind." He paused.

"Anything you need to say, you can say in front of Hannah. She is like Hope's second mother. Our daughters grew up together and practically lived at each other's houses before we moved here."

Hannah slipped in beside Amanda and took her hand.

"Ms. Ellis, I know you're wondering why I'm here instead of the officers who came last night. The evidence they collected gave them enough concern to bring me onto the case. I have some news."

Hannah held Amanda's hand tighter.

"Go on." Amanda looked at Hannah for reassurance.

"Ms. Ellis, it appears Hope was raped."

"Raped!" Amanda jumped up from her seat. "When? Who? How do you know?" She began pacing. "I don't think I can take much more of this."

The officer gave her a minute to gain her composure, and when he did, a wave of memories washed over Amanda. *Of course. All the showers and vomiting; I thought it was nerves. Sleeping on the couch. The way she asked for a security system and was neurotic about locking the doors.* Amanda sank back into the chair and held her head up with her fist. "Go on."

"It was in her diary. We don't know who, but it appears to have happened sometime close to your relocation. All of the entries before the incident were filled with adventures she had with a friend named Sydney."

"That's my daughter. They're best friends."

"Well, from then on, she begins writing about 'him,' although we don't know who that is. She talks about the incident taking place in her bedroom and how she can't sleep in that bed because she feels dirty just being in her room. She wrote about making up reasons to sleep on the sofa all summer long."

"I think I know who it was," she whispered, then louder, "Why didn't she tell me?" Amanda broke. With her face in her hands, she sobbed.

"In most rape cases, the assailant threatens the victim or her family members. It could be that she didn't tell you because he told her if she did he'd hurt her again, or you. Mind manipulation is a powerful weapon, Ms. Ellis."

Amanda held her hand up, needing a moment to process all he was telling her. "I'm sorry to have to question you after telling you this, but time is critical. I need to learn all I can to help us find your daughter. Officer White said you're divorced. When was the last time your daughter saw her father?"

"Charlie may be useless, and he disappeared before the ink dried on the divorce papers, but he wouldn't have done this. It was that weasel mover, Troy, I'd bet my life on it. Or the other one, James. But Troy kept talking about Hope, and he stopped by a few times to drop off flyers, then flowers. I wish I'd saved that answering machine message."

"Are there any other men she has been around unsupervised to your knowledge?"

"Not that I can think of."

He put his pen down. "Are you seeing anyone?"

"No, I don't date. I don't have any male friends. Neither does Hope. I don't think she even has any male teachers." Amanda threw her hands in the air, "Her bus driver is a woman!"

"What is it, Hannah? You look like you've seen a ghost."

"Amanda, I should've just stayed home that day. We have four years to take Sydney to visit colleges. Ed's so hung up on Asbury because he went there. I can't believe we just left her."

Amanda began to tremble. What had they done? How had she missed this?

"What do you know about Troy and James?" Detective Johnson asked.

"Someone I work with recommended them. It's two guys just starting their own business. They were cheaper than everyone else. I can't recall their last names. They sent me a card. Let me find it." Amanda walked out of the room still trembling.

"How could we have let this happen?" Hannah faced Detective Johnson, waiting for an answer.

"You have to cut yourself some slack, Mrs. Clarkston. This isn't your fault. It's not Ms. Ellis's either."

Amanda returned and thrust the card at Detective Johnson. Her blotchy face had twisted into rage. "Here it is. Troy Jackson and James Bullard. These numbers should be their cell phones."

"I'll go question them now. The more time that passes, the lower our chances are of finding Hope."

Amanda began to cry. "Hope convinced me she could stay home and wait for the movers so I wouldn't have to take off work. What kind of mother am I?"

Hannah held Amanda as she cried. "You're a wonderful mother and this is not your fault."

"Ms. Ellis, people like this prey on innocent victims. You had no way of knowing Hope was in danger. Besides, we don't know for sure if they are the ones Hope wrote about. I promise to keep you in the loop." The detective laid his hands on the table. "I know Officer Carlson showed you the marijuana he found in Hope's room. When I questioned Hope's friend, Nikki, she admitted that they smoked together. She said it helped Hope with the stress she was under but she wouldn't elaborate. If you think of anything—even if it seems insignificant—call me. The more we learn, the closer we'll be to finding Hope. Here's my card. I'll be in touch."

"Thank you, detective."

"I'll walk you out." Hannah stood and walked Detective Johnson to the door.

"Wait!" Amanda called out. "What were you doing up at the school?"

Detective Johnson shot her a questioning look. "Checking up on me?" He smiled.

"You were taking so long, I thought I should at least call the school and find out what classes Hope missed yesterday. The secretary said something about a note."

He pulled out his notes. "Yes, the attendance office had a note from her father stating she had an appointment. I think it was forged."

"So what does that mean? Do you think someone came to the school and checked her out?"

"I'm not sure what it means other than Hope left the high school by choice. What happened after that is anyone's guess at this point. Are you sure there isn't someone she's been involved with recently?"

"Not that I know of, but apparently a lot has been going on that I don't know about." She shook her head. "I just want Hope home where she belongs."

"I will do everything I can to make that happen, Ms. Ellis. I'll be in touch."

CHAPTER 21

Destiny stood on the porch with her back turned to the door. Hope could hear her talking, though she couldn't make out anything specific. Still, she glared over her shoulder, straight at Hope. *Probably wants to make sure I'm still sitting in the chair,* Hope thought. She wanted to scream loud enough for the person on the other end of Destiny's conversation to hear her. But before she got her nerve up, Destiny walked back in.

"Come on, we've got to get this finished. T called. He's hosting tonight, so you've got to be ready."

"What do you mean T is hosting?"

Destiny didn't respond to the question. Instead, she pulled Hope's head down into the sink to finish what she started. Hope complied as Destiny moved quickly through the washing and rinsing. After the blow dry, she used some kind of styling gel before pulling and tugging the hair in different directions. When she was finished, Destiny piled all the supplies back under the sink—except the scissors. Hope never saw them again.

"Can I see it?"

Destiny handed her a small mirror.

Hope gasped. She didn't recognize the person staring back at her. She fingered the cherry red layers of her new 'do.

"I don't look like myself."

"That's the idea." Destiny grabbed the mirror and shoved it back under the sink.

"With a look like that, we've gotta get you a new name. Don't ever let T hear you telling people your name is Hope ever again. From now on, your name is Cherry."

"What are you talking about? Why would I lie?"

"Girl, when are you going to get it through that pretty little head of yours nothing is like it used to be? You're not going back. You're one of T's girls now. Hope died last night and Cherry was born. From now on, you're Cherry to everybody, even yourself."

"What if I don't want to be one of T's girls? What if I want to go home to my mom?"

"Your mom . . . your mom is the reason you're gonna stay, girl. If you don't do exactly what T say, your mom's the one who's gonna pay the price. T won't hesitate to hurt her or anyone else he needs to, so you best stay in line. You hear me? You best just do what he say."

Destiny walked out of the room leaving Hope alone to worry. She stroked the ends of her hair. Would T really hurt her mom? Did he know where she lived? Had she told him her last name? Then she remembered: the note. He had her. He knew who she was, where she went to school, and most likely where she lived. Hope was trapped. She couldn't do anything about her situation except watch it play out. But she could protect her mom, and she would do whatever was necessary.

Hope wandered out to the living room where she found Destiny.

"You smoke?" she asked, blowing smoke circles in Hope's direction.

"Never cigarettes, only a joint." Hope looked down at the ground, embarrassed to admit it.

"So there is a little wild child in you?" Destiny smiled up at her. "That will come in handy, make it easier for you."

Make what easier? Hope thought, but she chose not to ask right now. She wasn't sure she wanted to know the answer.

"T's hosting tonight. That means he'll have some men come by for a little party. You and me will help T entertain the men."

"What do you mean, entertain? Are we supposed to make food and serve them?"

"Oh, we'll serve them, all right. We'll serve them any way they want. And if you do a good job, T will reward you."

Hope didn't know exactly how he would reward her, but maybe he'd let her go home or at least call her mom.

"Help me get this place picked up so we're ready when T gets here." Destiny put her cigarette out and went into the kitchen.

More beer and liquor bottles littered the room, as well as food wrappers. Destiny dragged in a trashcan. She and Hope cleaned everything up and straightened what little furniture there was.

When Destiny gave her fresh sheets and told her to change her bed, a cold chill ran down Hope's spine. Destiny had called the bed and the room hers. She wanted no part of it, and as soon as she could find a way out, she was going to take it. Maybe she could slip some information to one of the men who came to the party tonight. If they could let her mom know where she was, then she would come get her.

Destiny walked in the room just as Hope finished making the bed. She had her arms loaded with clothes.

"Here." She dropped the pile on the bed. "Try these on and let me see each outfit. We have to find something for you to wear tonight."

Hope took the clothes and kicked the door shut so she could change. Destiny laughed as she went back to the living room.

Hope held up the first dress. It looked like it might be too small. But she wedged herself into it. The hem sat less than an inch below her butt, and it fit like a glove across her chest, leaving nothing to the imagination. There was no way she would be caught dead in something so provocative. The next outfit wasn't any better.

"Destiny, none of these are going to work. I look like a tramp in all of them."

And then it clicked. This wasn't going to be a party. This was a business and she was the product. The color drained from her face as she slid down to the floor. Her whole body shook.

"So, you finally figured things out." Destiny stood in the doorway. "It took you long enough. Now you do what you're told and no one will hurt you. T doesn't allow the men to beat his girls. When the men get here, you follow my lead. We'll sit with them, dance with them, and possibly even dance for them. When one of them takes you by the hand and asks where your room is, you lead him in here and do whatever he says. If he walks out happy, then T is happy. If T is happy, then things will go well for you. You got it? Any trouble out of you and it will be trouble for you."

"I can't do this." Hope's voice hardly swelled above a whisper.

"You ain't got no choice. None of us do."

Destiny looked away and sighed. Hope realized Destiny wasn't in charge of anything. She was simply assigned the task of getting Hope ready. Their fate was the same.

"Destiny?" Hope ran her hand across her cheek. "What's your real name?"

"Girl, Destiny is the only name I have. It's the only name anyone ever needs to know. That other girl, she died a long time ago." She looked away as a tear fell. She turned to go. "You better pick one of those out because T will be by in a little while to make sure you're ready. If he ain't happy with you, then both of us will pay the price."

CHAPTER 22

Hope winced. She didn't want Destiny to be in trouble with T. She was the closest thing to a friend she'd have as long as she was held here. With a deep sigh, Hope sorted through the outfits and picked the one she found least offensive. It was tight and it was short, but at least you couldn't see through it. She put it on and walked into the living room where Destiny waited.

"Well?"

"Not bad. The black makes your hair look really red. I think T will like it. Now let's get you some shoes. What size do you wear?"

"Six." Where was Destiny going to find a size six shoe to match this outfit without leaving the house? Did she have a special stash somewhere?

Within minutes, Destiny returned from another room carrying a pair of black high-heeled boots.

"This is all I got right now. Try them on and see if you can walk in them without falling down." The heels were at least four inches tall; the boots would come above Hope's knees.

She put them on and stood up. She took a few steps, which seemed to satisfy Destiny.

"Okay, take it all off for now. We need to eat lunch and get some sleep so we're ready for tonight."

Hope hadn't taken a nap during the day since she was in preschool. How in the world could she sleep knowing what was going to happen to her later that night? She didn't think she could even eat, though her growling stomach said otherwise. Hope slipped back into her jeans while Destiny pulled some things together for lunch.

"Cherry, you like peanut butter?"

Hope looked around the room, uncomfortable with the new name. "Yeah, thanks."

"You know, Cherry, I'm not your enemy here."

Hope looked at her.

"You need to get used to responding to Cherry. Hope is gone forever."

"You can say that again."

They finished their sandwiches and cleaned up the kitchen.

"Here." Destiny handed Hope a pill.

"What's this?"

"It will help you sleep. Between being nervous and the daylight, it's hard to nap sometimes. You'll get used to it, but for now this will help you."

Hope looked at the small pill in her hand.

Destiny handed her a glass of water. "Look at it this way. You'll go to sleep as Hope and wake up Cherry."

Hope was willing to take anything that would knock her out and let her escape for a bit. She swallowed the pill and walked into the room they called hers. Destiny told her to try and go straight to sleep. She would wake her in time to get ready.

Hope looked for a lock as she closed the door, but found none. She remembered the deadbolt on the closet door and shivered. Climbing into bed she rolled on her side. She could hear Destiny talking to someone and thought she might go see who it was. But before she could throw the sheet back she was fast asleep.

* * *

"She ready?"

"Yeah, she's ready. She's scared to death, T, but she's ready." Destiny questioned whether she was cut out to groom new girls. Hope seemed so sweet. Destiny wished she could help Hope escape, but she was just as much a prisoner. If she couldn't help her escape, she would help her survive.

"Look, girl, I told you being the bottom wasn't always an easy job, but you wanted it. I can throw you back on the track or put you back at the ranch if this is too much for you."

T's words jolted her back to reality. "No, T, I can do it. It's just this is my first time. I won't let you down."

"I knew you wouldn't." He pulled her close and kissed her. "That's why I bought you this." He handed her a box.

She opened it and found a blue dress inside. It was classy, not like what she usually wore.

"Oh, T, it's nice." She looked up at him, her smile almost making its way into her eyes.

"That ain't no working dress, girl. That's for you to wear for me when we go somewhere special. If tonight goes well, you might just have to wear it for me when I take you out. I gotta roll. I'll be by around eight or so. You make sure you're both ready. Go over the rules with her. By the way, what did you name her?"

"Cherry, to match her bright red hair."

* * *

At seven o'clock Destiny woke Cherry. "Time to get up. You've got to eat something and then we have to get you ready."

Hope thought Destiny seemed different, barking orders at her. Why had things changed? She did as she was told.

"There's soup in the kitchen. You don't want to eat too much before your first time. You'll get sick."

She dragged herself out of bed and into the kitchen. She started sipping the soup when Destiny held out another pill.

"This will help you wake up."

Hope swallowed what she was given and washed out her bowl. Then she hurried into the bathroom. Straining for a glimpse of daylight, she pulled herself up to look out the high window. More bars. How was she going to make it through this night?

A knock at the door interrupted her daydreaming.

"Let's go, girl. I gotta do your makeup."

Hope complied.

"Sit down. This time I'll do it for you. Eventually, you'll have to learn how to fix it the way T likes it." Destiny rested a hand on Hope's shoulder. "It helps if you think of yourself as someone else. You look so different from who you used to be." Hope caught a glimmer of Destiny's tenderness before she swirled the eye shadow brush around in the blue powder till it looked like a hydrangea.

Hope had wanted to learn to wear makeup, but not like this. *Snap out of it,* she thought, nearly out loud. Seriously, she had to stop thinking about what Hope used to do and think about what Cherry would do or she would never survive. Cherry's edgy look required a lot of makeup. She would wear clothes that fit tight without underwear. Cherry was reckless. *I must begin to think like Cherry, dress like Cherry, be Cherry, no matter what, for Mom's sake.* T had already destroyed Hope, but she couldn't let him hurt her mom.

When Destiny finished with Cherry's makeup, she told her to get dressed and meet her in the living room.

Hope walked out feeling dirty already and the men hadn't even arrived yet.

"You look good." Destiny took a picture with her cell phone. She sent it to T.

"Listen girl, there are some rules you gotta follow. You do and you'll be all right. T wants us to call the men who come by tonight "baby" or "sugar." You don't tell the guy your name unless he asks you, and you never ask him what his name is. If you do, you'll pay for it later. No matter what he does to you, don't scream. If you do, you'll answer to T when the man leaves, and it won't be pretty. Got it?" Hope stared straight ahead, trying hard not to throw up on Destiny's boots.

"Hope, you with me?" Hope nodded.

Destiny continued, "The guy can do whatever he wants because he's paid for you. There are condoms in your room. You're allowed to offer them, but don't argue if he says no. He won't hit you, because he'll have to deal with T if he does. T don't want no bruises or cuts on his girls. When the guy's finished, he'll get dressed and leave. You get dressed and if the sheets are ruined, change them. There are new sheets in the closet."

Hope looked at the closet door. Nothing had been in the closet earlier. What else had gone on while she was asleep?

"Girl, pay attention! If the sheets are clean, then just make the bed. When you finish making the bed, you come back out and sit down until someone motions you over. You may be young, but you know how to flirt, girl. You did it with T. Just do the same thing with the men. Don't act like a scared little girl or T will give you a reason to be scared. If you do your job, nobody will hurt you. If you come out the bedroom and no one is waiting, you know you're done for the night and you can go to bed. Got it?"

"I can't do this, Destiny." Tears puddled in Hope's eyes. Everything in her was trembling. She felt bile rise up in her throat.

"You ain't got no choice. None of us do. Your life depends on it and so does your mama's. The best thing you can do is don't think. Just do what you're told and you'll be OK. Now get it together before you mess up your makeup."

The sadness in Destiny's eyes told Hope she spoke from experience. The mention of her mother caused Hope to sit down. Her mother had already been hurt so much. First her dad left with another woman, then they had to move, and now Hope was gone. She would do whatever she had to do to protect her mother's life. It was the least she could do.

Destiny turned some music on and went into the kitchen. She came back with a bottle of beer and a pill.

"Take it. It will help you do what you have to do and survive it."

Hope took the pill and washed it down with the beer. She gagged and handed it back to Destiny.

"Keep it. You'll need it."

Destiny swallowed her own pill and downed the remainder of her beer. Just then the back door opened and T walked in with a trail of men behind him.

"Hey, hey!" he said. "The party has arrived, ladies."

He walked up to Hope and ran his eyes over her body. He gave her a kiss on the cheek and whispered in her ear. "Saw your mama today and she looked real sad. Don't cause her any more pain, girl."

He turned around to the men and smiled.

"Didn't I tell you I added something sweet to the menu? Who wants to be first?"

His laugh sounded like the devil.

The men all looked her up and down just as T had done. Hope swallowed hard thinking of what was about to happen. *Don't think. You'll survive this if you listen to Destiny and just don't think.* She could feel the drugs kicking in just as a man stepped forward and took her hand. He looked at her like a hungry animal that hadn't eaten in days. He twirled her around and leaned in close. He pulled her up against his body hard, grabbed her butt and squeezed it so hard it stung. He ran his tongue down her neck and then laughed.

"Yeah, she's real sweet. I have a big sweet tooth tonight and need me some sugar. I'll go first." He slid money into T's hand without taking his eyes off of Hope. He pulled her by the hand back to the bedroom. He seemed to know right where to go. This was it. She was a prisoner in the pit of hell and there was no way out.

CHAPTER 23

Amanda woke to ringing in her ear. It took a moment for her to realize it was her phone. She jumped from the sofa and ran into the kitchen. *Oh, God, please let it be Hope, and please don't let her hang up.*

"Hello!" She almost screamed into the phone.

"Ms. Ellis, this is Detective Johnson. Is everything all right?"

"No, nothing is right, Detective Johnson. Not unless you're calling me to tell me you've found Hope and you're bringing her home."

"I'm sorry. I haven't found your daughter, but I have some new information and wondered if I could come by."

She looked at the mess in the kitchen. "Come on over."

"I'll be there in twenty minutes."

Amanda hung the phone up and methodically began loading the dishwasher and making coffee. How long had she been asleep? The last thing she remembered was pushing Hannah out the door, sending her home to her family for the night.

Amanda had spent hours going through Hope's room, looking for any clue the police might have overlooked. When she came across Hope's baby book, she sobbed so hard her shoulders and chest still hurt. She fell asleep clinging to the scrapbook. It helped her feel close to Hope.

She opened the door. Detective Johnson looked exhausted.

121

"Good morning, Ms. Ellis."

"Come in. I just made coffee. Would you like a cup?"

"I'd appreciate it. It's been a long night." He followed her into the kitchen. Taking the mug she handed him, he took a seat at the table. He sat a few moments without saying anything.

Amanda couldn't take the silence anymore. "What is it? I can take it; just tell me."

"We found Troy and James but can only hold them for twenty-four hours without pressing charges. They are denying any knowledge of a rape. They told me they left the house together and didn't return until Troy stopped by to drop off the business cards with you. We've questioned your neighbors, and no one remembers seeing anyone in your driveway that day other than the moving van. All we have to go on is Hope's journal, and that's just not enough to press charges. I'm sorry."

"What if I want to press charges? Hope's a minor."

"I'm sorry, Ms. Ellis. Even if you did, there is no conclusive evidence. It would just mean that they'd get off, and we couldn't prosecute them after we find Hope. We'll be able to do that with her testimony. For what it's worth, I don't think Troy or James know where she is now. In fact, it's my gut feeling they didn't have anything to do with her disappearance."

Amanda was grateful for Detective Johnson's straightforwardness.

He continued, "We know from what Nikki said and from what we found in her room that Hope was using. Marijuana is usually the starting point. She might have tried other things. Now that I've run into a dead end with the movers, I'm going to question everyone she knew and see where that leads us."

"She took MARTA after school every day to volunteer at the public library not far from here. She worked until dinnertime. Ms. Joyce drove her home two days a week, and she rode MARTA on Mondays, Wednesdays, and Fridays."

Johnson wrote notes on his pad. "Did she ever mention anyone she might have met at the library or on the train?"

"No, no one other than Nikki. And there was a boy called Blake, though she only mentioned him once or twice."

"I'll talk with Nikki again and visit the librarian to see what she can tell me. If Hope left the library at the same time every Monday, Wednesday, and Friday it will help. Then I can ride MARTA a few days to question the regulars."

"Thank you, detective." Amanda got up to refill her coffee.

"If you think of anything else, please let me know. Based on the evidence we have right now, the trail to follow is drug-related. A lot of times young girls will turn to drugs as a coping mechanism when they've been raped or abused. I know that isn't what you want to hear, but it is obvious Hope left school on her own free will. Whoever she left with was someone who made her feel safe. We just need to determine who it was, and that may lead us to her." He stood up to leave. "Don't worry, Ms. Ellis. I'll find Hope. It may take time, but I won't give up until I find her."

Amanda stood at the door watching him back out of the driveway. She couldn't imagine her girl using drugs. Or being raped. The tears began to fall, but she wiped them away. She couldn't give in. She had to stay strong and do whatever she could to help Detective Johnson find Hope. She reached for the phone to update Hannah.

"Hello."

"Hannah? Detective Johnson came by today and said there wasn't enough evidence to hold the movers. Right now it's their word against Hope's diary since Hope isn't present to give a statement. He feels in his gut the movers had nothing to do with her disappearance. He thinks it has to do with drugs."

"Drugs? Why does he think drugs?"

"Well, they did find the marijuana in her room, and Nikki confirmed it was Hope's. They smoked it together in the afternoons. Oh, Hannah, I feel so stupid. I came home a couple of times and smelled smoke on Hope. When I questioned her about it, she always had an explanation."

"You can't beat yourself up over this. You're a good mom and you had no reason to ever doubt Hope. She's always been open and honest with you. Have you heard anything from Charlie?"

"He called, but a lot of good that did. He told me to keep him posted. For God's sake, this is his daughter and all he could say is 'keep me posted.' I can't believe he's the man I was married to all those years. It's a good thing he's several states away or I might've strangled him. I know he left me, but I never thought he'd just write off Hope like that too."

"Don't let him get to you, Amanda. Did you get any sleep last night?"

"Yeah, I fell asleep on the sofa. But what am I going to do? I can't just sit here. I'll lose my job. I can't work either. What if Hope tries to call me and I'm not home?"

"Listen, I've already called the church. The pastors and elders have decided to cover your bills for the month so you can take a leave of absence and focus on finding Hope. If they don't cover everything, just let me and Ed know. We'll make up the difference."

"You can't do that, Hannah. I won't let you."

"Amanda, for heaven's sake, she grew up in my house as much as she did yours. We love Hope like she's ours. Please let us do this for you. It's all we know to do, and we have to do something."

Silence hung on the line for a few moments. For the first time since Charlie left, Amanda didn't feel alone.

"Thank you," she said in a whisper. "This means so much more than you'll ever know. How's Sydney doing?"

"She feels like she failed Hope as a friend. It breaks her heart to know Hope was raped and didn't feel like she could tell her. She's bound and determined to find a way to help. She told us not to buy her anything for Christmas but to use the money to run an ad in the paper with Hope's picture, asking if anyone has seen her. She put your number and Detective Johnson's number on a flyer she made on the computer last night. She said having Hope home safe and sound is all she wants for Christmas."

"Why didn't I think of making posters? Hug Sydney for me and please tell her she is the best friend Hope has ever had. She did not let Hope down; I did."

"You didn't let her down either. Do you want me to come over?"

"No, I think I'll call the phone company. I'm going to see if they can forward all of the home phone calls to my cell so I won't have to stay in the house. I have to do something. I am going to go talk to Ms. Joyce at the library. Someone has to remember something they haven't told Detective Johnson."

* * *

Amanda walked into the library in the middle of story time. She smiled to see all the little kids, but wanted to shout to the other parents, "Hold them tight! Never take their safety for granted." Joyce saw Amanda and nodded in her direction. She stopped midway through *Ira Sleeps Over* to say, "Excuse me, children. A very special guest is here. Do you remember Hope from summer?" Cheers of joy came from the kids, and fond smiles crossed parents' faces. "This is her mother. I know Ms. Ellis is glad that you all love Hope. Come over here, Ms. Ellis."

Amanda shook her head, tears starting to collect in her eye sockets, and motioned for Joyce to speak to her privately.

"Oh, I see. I'm sorry, children. Ms. Ellis needs to tell me something. Mrs. Chronister, will you finish reading?"

Joyce made her way to Amanda, who was barely holding it together. She took Amanda's hand and led her into the library's office.

"Have a seat, dear. You look upset. What's wrong? How can I help?"

"Hope is missing."

"Missing?"

"She didn't come home from school on Wednesday. The police are looking for her, but all the leads are going nowhere."

"Oh my. What can I do?"

"Did Hope seem strange to you? Did she say anything about anything at all?"

"I noticed she looked thin, and she seemed distracted, but I just thought it was the stress of moving and high school and changing schools. You know, girls that age need their privacy. I didn't want to pry. She was so diligent about that science project, I thought things must be going very well for the two of you."

Amanda offered a weak smile, "Thank you for giving her a safe haven."

"Hope was a joy to have around. I can say this and mean it, it was very much my pleasure." A tear appeared at Joyce's eye. "Thank you. That means a lot."

"Please let me know when she comes home, and promise if there's anything I can do, you'll let me know?"

"Of course. Thanks, Joyce." Amanda stared into space for a moment. "Oh, and do you think some of Hope's friends could hang a poster here with Hope's picture?"

"Certainly."

CHAPTER 24

It seemed like the room of men would never empty. Hope was exhausted. Her body raged in pain. She craved sleep. Fear kept her from closing the door behind one of the men as he left and curling up to sleep. Just as the sun came up, she walked into the living room to see only T sitting there.

"You done good, baby girl. You done real good." He sat there counting his money. "Now go get some sleep, 'cause Destiny will have you up soon cleaning this place for our next party."

"We have another one already?" Hope reached deep into herself for a shred of strength. "No. I'm not doing it."

T shot Destiny a warning look.

"Shut up, Cherry." Destiny said. She slapped Hope across the face. Hope touched her flaming red cheek. "Next time it'll be worse."

T nodded. "Girl, we party every night. You'll get used to it. Now go to bed. You look like hell." He left the living room, but before he got to the door, he spun on his heel and looked at Hope. "I'm letting you off this time. It's your first day, and I'm feeling generous. If you ever say no to me again, I'll hurt you bad, then I'll kill your mama." T walked out the back door.

Hope crumpled onto the floor.

"Get up." Destiny grabbed her under the arm.

"Why?"

"You need some rest, and I'm sick of looking at you."

Hope walked to the bathroom and turned the shower on as hot as she could stand it and climbed in. She scrubbed her skin raw trying to wash off the filth. Didn't those men know she was someone's daughter? Several of them wore wedding rings. *Why weren't they home with their families? Where were their wives? Did they have daughters?* The questions rushed through her mind. She fell in a heap and began to vomit. She finally pulled herself together and got cleaned up. Her entire body ached. She wasn't sure how she would ever be able to sleep. As she opened the bathroom door, she was startled to see Destiny standing there with her own tear-streaked face.

Another pill. "This will help you go to sleep."

Hope reached for it, hesitant.

"It's the only way you'll find sleep. Trust me, girl. I know what I'm talking about."

Hope swallowed the pill and went to her room. There were clean sheets on the bed. She turned to say thank you as the bathroom door closed. She turned back around and practically fell into the bed.

The next thing she knew, Destiny was shaking her. Another pill. "This will help you wake up. It's time to get the house clean." It seemed as though she'd only been asleep a few minutes. Hope groaned. Everything in her hurt. She took the pill.

And so the routine was established. Take one pill to wake up, one pill to lose the inhibitions, and another to go to sleep. Most of the pills she washed down with alcohol of some form or another. Hope didn't care that she'd never drunk liquor before. She didn't care that the only drug she had ever done before was pot. She was in survival mode. She would swallow whatever would make her mind and body numb. If she was lucky, it just might kill her.

After two solid weeks of T's so-called parties, T walked in the door in the early afternoon. He was alone.

"You've earned yourself an afternoon off. Destiny is going to take you to get your nails done and maybe even get a new outfit. Don't do anything stupid or you'll regret it, you hear?"

"Can I call my mom to say hello?" She knew what the answer would be but thought it wouldn't hurt to ask.

"Hell, no! You ain't calling nobody! If anybody asks you who you are or why you ain't in school, you just tell 'em you're from out of town visiting your friend Destiny. Then you keep quiet and let Destiny do the talking. She knows the drill. I'll meet you back here at eight o'clock. You better be wearing your new outfit so I can see what I bought. Make sure it's sexy."

Hope didn't say anything. She stared at the ground.

"You hear me, girl?" T shouted.

"Yes, sir."

T laughed so loud it made her ears ring.

"You hear that, Destiny? She called me 'sir.' I'm glad somebody around here knows her place." He laughed all the way out the door.

"Put on your clothes. I'll get you some shoes to wear and we'll go. It looks like he gave me enough money for us to eat at McDonald's too."

Hope dressed quickly and was ready in no time. This would be the first time she got out of the house since the day she walked in with T. She couldn't wait to smell the fresh air and see other people.

Destiny tossed her some shoes and a sweatshirt, and they were off. The first stop was the nail salon. Destiny told the ladies they both wanted long red nails. Hope would have preferred to have hers short, but she knew better than to question Destiny.

This was the first time someone had touched her in several weeks without demanding something from her. She closed her eyes and remembered a time when she and Sydney spent the day with their moms at Perimeter Mall shopping and going out to lunch. They topped off the day at the nail salon.

"Did I hurt you?" The nail technician looked alarmed.

Hope opened her eyes and found the technician looking at her.

"Oh, no, you didn't hurt me."

"Why you cry then?"

Destiny shot her a warning look.

"I'm not crying . . . I just got some of the dust in my eye from the filing." She smiled at the girl.

The door to the nail salon barely closed before Destiny went off. "What the hell were you trying to pull in there?"

"I'm sorry. When I closed my eyes I got homesick. I won't do it again."

"See that you don't. We don't need nobody getting suspicious. If T lets us out the house, don't you mess it up for us."

They walked down the sidewalk to a clothing store where Destiny picked out some things for Hope to try on. She wouldn't have been caught dead in any of these before. She turned to look at herself in the mirror. Well, Hope wouldn't wear anything like this, but Cherry would. Cherry would wear it and even worse, she thought. Destiny looked at all of the outfits and decided the eggplant-colored dress would please T. She chose a yellow dress for herself.

"Don't make eye contact with the lady at the checkout. Keep your eyes down and let me do the talking." Destiny pulled out a wad of cash.

The girl was on the phone when they arrived at the counter. She rang them up, bagged their things and sent them on their way without pausing from her conversation.

"We got just enough money to go to McDonald's, but it will have to be fast. We have to be back at the house in an hour or we face punishment." Destiny seemed to fear T as much as Hope did.

"Destiny, I thought you were T's partner. Why are you afraid of him?" Hope crammed French fries in her mouth.

"Girl, T ain't got no partner, unless you consider Slick Rick his partner. They cousins, so they pull their herds together sometimes. But T works alone."

"Herds?"

"Yeah, you know, girls. Me and you and the others."

Hope stopped walking. "There are others?"

"Now I done talked too much. C'mon, we gotta go." Destiny avoided eye contact with Hope.

"Come on, Destiny, tell me what you're talking about. You're the closest thing to a friend I have."

"Girl, ain't none of us got friends in this hell. I'm just like you. I'm one of T's girls. I only get to train because I'm the bottom."

"The bottom?" Hope was confused.

"You know, the bottom whore. It's my job to train you. When this week's over, T's gonna move you to the ranch with the rest of the herd to make room for a new girl."

Hope's appetite disappeared. There were others, and others would be brought in, tricked just like her. Where was T going to take her? Would she ever see Destiny again? How would she survive this?

"Let's go. T's expecting us in thirty minutes. We gotta get home and get ready." Destiny shoved the last of her hamburger into her mouth.

They walked the rest of the way without saying a word.

As they approached the back door of the house, Destiny grabbed Hope's arm. "Look, don't you breathe a word of what I told you. T would beat me bad if he knew I let it slip. I just didn't want you to get caught off guard."

"I won't say a thing. Promise." Hope followed Destiny in the house.

"Hurry up and get dressed. Do you think you can do your own makeup or do you need my help?"

"I can do it."

"Okay, but make sure you do a lot of mascara and eyeliner. T likes us real made up."

Hope went into the bathroom and wiggled into her skimpy new dress. She stared at the barrage of makeup sitting on the counter. She dabbed foundation on her already clear complexion. Noticing darkness underneath her eyes, she dabbed a little more in that area. Next she picked up the mascara. Ultra, extra black.

Perfect.

With shaking hands, she brushed a layer on her left eyelashes then switched to the right ones. She needed more, jammed the brush back into the container and applied a second coat. The mascara became so thick it almost blurred her vision. That was okay. She didn't want to see anyway.

The eyeliner was tricky. Her thick lines were kind of squiggly when she finished, but it would do. She smeared the shadow brush into smoky eye shadow as she completed the transformation from Hope to Cherry.

Next, she brushed hot pink blush on her cheeks. She kept blinking, trying to get used to the weight of the makeup. She spotted a tube of red lip gloss. She squeezed some on her finger, and brushed her lips with the ruby, shimmery gloss.

Placing it back on the counter, she never took her gaze off of the image in the mirror. Nothing about it resembled Hope in any way, except maybe the sad eyes. Hope wasn't staring back at her. Cherry was.

Her hands trembled as she smoothed her dress. Taking one last glance at her appearance, she spied bare feet.

"Destiny! Shoes! I need some shoes!" She yelled down the hall.

"I put the black boots in your room. They'll look good with your dress. T will be impressed."

After zipping the boots, Cherry walked to the bedroom where Destiny was finishing up her makeup.

"How do I look?"

Destiny looked up from the mirror. "Damn, girl, you look so good, T might just keep you for himself tonight." Just then the back door opened. It was party time.

CHAPTER 25

"T's early. Hurry up and turn the music on." Destiny went storming out of the bedroom.

Cherry wasn't sure which way to turn. "What about my pill?"

T walked into the living room alone. Cherry looked at Destiny, unsure of what was about to happen.

"We party at another destination tonight. There's a man who requested both of you."

He turned to Cherry. "Your mama went back to work today. She looked good. If you play by the rules tonight, she'll go to work tomorrow, if you get my drift." His eyes spoke more evil than his mouth. Cherry would do whatever she needed to do to keep her mom safe. Her life might be over, but her mom wouldn't be hurt.

"I'll play by the rules, T. Just tell me what to do."

"That's my girl." He grabbed her and kissed her hard. "Damn, girl, you look so good, I wish I could keep you tonight, but business is business and this man is paying big. He's having a little gathering in his suite before the game. You ladies are the entertainment for his guests. Make sure they're pleased."

Cherry looked at Destiny. She nodded.

They rode in T's Suburban to a hotel. Cherry never knew T had a car. Why did he ride MARTA all the time if he had a car?

They arrived at the hotel in downtown Atlanta and T parked.

"Look, he gave me a key, so there is no need to even slow down in the lobby. We don't need any attention. Just walk through the door to the elevator. Destiny, you know the room. I'll be waiting in the car when you're done."

When they got in the elevator, Destiny turned to Cherry. "Remember, you don't ask their names, you just call them 'sugar' or 'baby.' Do this right and we get to go to bed early because this is a big job. T's making more money than any party we've had since you came. Make one mistake and it's both our asses."

Cherry nodded. Her heart pounded in her throat. When the elevator door opened, they found their way to the suite down a long hallway. Destiny used her key to get in. Cherry followed behind her. When the door closed, a deep voice announced, "Gentlemen, it appears your entertainment has arrived. Help yourselves."

*   *   *

Cherry's body throbbed as she made her way to the car. She didn't know evil like that existed. The men were mostly married bankers and lawyers, but that was only until the door closed. Then they became animals.

Destiny banged on the car door. T woke up and let the girls in. When Destiny handed T the money, he took time to count it before starting the car.

"Well, ladies, it looks like you've earned yourselves a trip to the Waffle House and an early night. Well done!"

Waffle House? Are you kidding me? All Cherry wanted to do was get in a hot shower and wash the smell of the men off her. She could still feel their hands on her. She sat in the backseat wishing she could die.

T whistled all the way to the Waffle House. He was in a good mood. Cherry knew eating out was a treat for them, so even though her stomach turned over at the thought of food, she made herself eat. The ride back to the house was quiet.

"Cherry, get you some sleep. Tomorrow you meet the rest of the herd. Later!" T walked out of the house whistling.

Cherry turned to Destiny. Now she was really scared. As awful as this place was, at least she knew the routine. That provided some comfort. She depended on Destiny. How would she survive without her?

"Will you be going with me?" Cherry's eyes were pleading.

"No, girl, I gotta stay here. T has another girl he's bringing in tomorrow night. I'll have to train her, just like you."

"How many of us are there?"

"I've lost count; somewhere around twelve, unless Rick lost another one of his to T. Rick likes to play cards with T but he loses more than he wins. He doesn't like to pay T money when he loses, so he pays him with girls."

"Where is he taking me?"

"You mean the ranch? T just calls it that because he keeps his herd there." Cherry began to pace as Destiny talked with her. "It's just an apartment complex down the road a ways."

"Will I see you again?"

"Yeah, if T don't have a girl for me to train, then I'll come down and visit you all. Now get some sleep. He'll expect you to be ready when he gets here tomorrow."

Hesitantly, Cherry walked up to Destiny and gave her a hug. "Thanks for shooting it straight with me."

At first Destiny was rigid, but then she gave in and hugged back. She let go quickly and walked into her room.

*　*　*

Cherry and Destiny were allowed to sleep in. T was to pick Cherry up at lunchtime, so she had to be ready.

"What do I take with me?"

"All you take is the blue dress he bought you yesterday. You earned it. You don't have to share it with anyone else. There will be a closet full of clothes at the ranch. When it's time to party, you pull from there. The only thing that's yours is what T buys you as a reward for good behavior. If you mess up, you lose it all to the closet. But that's the least of your worries if you mess up. Play by the rules, girl. I don't want nothing bad to happen to you."

Cherry couldn't help but laugh. Everything that had happened to her since she'd arrived had been bad.

T showed up right on time. Cherry wore the pair of jeans and T-shirt she was given the morning she met Destiny. She carried the blue dress over her arm. T didn't say anything on the ride, and Cherry didn't feel the need to talk. She tried to take in everything she could as they drove down the street. She recognized nothing. Cherry knew they were somewhere near downtown, but she had no idea where. It made her heart hurt to know she was so close to her mom and couldn't get to her. She might as well be in Japan.

T pulled into an apartment complex at the end of a street and parked. There were no cars in the lot, and the balconies were empty. It looked deserted. When T got out of the car and started up the sidewalk, Cherry followed. She looked for any sign of civilization along the way.

"Welcome to the Sweet T Ranch." T held his arms out wide.

He unlocked a downstairs apartment and held the door for Cherry to walk through. She held her breath. Everything was dark.

"The girls are all asleep. They had a long night last night, with the game in town and all. You'll meet them soon enough."

"How many are there?"

T raised his hand and smacked her across the face; the force of it threw her into the wall. Her jaw felt like something had exploded inside and she tasted blood. Destiny had warned her he could be violent, but Cherry hadn't seen it. She certainly didn't want to see it again.

"Girl, you know better than to ask questions. You just listen and do as you're told. You hear me?" T's hot breath poured down over her face.

At first she was afraid to speak, but he was waiting for a response. "Yes, sir," Cherry managed to squeak out. The manners were habit.

"That's right! You call me 'sir' and you do what you're told."

He banged on the door down the hall. It opened and there stood a girl about Cherry's age with golden hair spilling across her shoulders.

"Get out here and meet your new roommate." T pulled the girl into the hallway.

She wore a pair of boxers that hung on her and a sloppy T-shirt. Except for the setting, she could have been any teenager who'd woken up too early on a Saturday morning. She looked Cherry up and down with questioning eyes.

"This here is Honey," T said. "She's dripping with sweetness." He pulled her up against his body in a possessive way. He looked like he was going to kiss her, but instead he grabbed a handful of her hair and slung her in front of Cherry. "Meet Cherry, my latest acquisition."

Honey nodded. Cherry was afraid to speak. She was afraid to move. From the moment they arrived at the apartment complex, she saw the vilest side of T. She wanted to do whatever was necessary to stay on his good side.

"Honey will show you the closet. Be ready to party by six o'clock. Anyone who isn't ready on time goes into lockup." T walked out and locked the door behind him.

The girls stood in silence, studying each other before anyone spoke.

"Does anyone else live here?" Cherry wiped blood from the corner of her mouth.

"Not in this apartment. I got moved here so you wouldn't be in here alone."

Cherry froze, still as a statue. "Where did you get moved from?"

"Just another apartment. What is this, twenty questions?"

"Excuse me for being curious, but I'm trying to figure out what's going on here."

"What's going on here? I'll tell you what's going on. T calls this his ranch; I call it hell. It's been abandoned for a long time so no one comes down this road until the sun goes down. Each apartment has at least two girls in it, or so we've been told. No one really knows how many girls T has at a time."

Honey fell into a chair like a deflated balloon. "Every night starting at sundown so many customers come through those doors, they nearly fall off their hinges. Some nights we see thirty men each, like last night. If we're lucky, we only have to endure ten or fifteen before T comes and locks up for the night. If you mess up, you get locked up, and I don't mean you get the night off."

Cherry tried to take it all in, but Honey wasn't finished with the tirade.

"He locks you in a tiny closet with the roaches and the rats and leaves you there, sometimes for days. It's cold and damp. You never know when he's coming back or if he's coming back. Part of you hopes he won't so you can just die. That's what's going on. Now, I'm sorry I'm not up to entertaining company right now. I just got off work an hour ago and I'm beat. The closet in the hall has clothes in it. Be ready at six o'clock or you pay the price. Everyone's on their own around here, so don't look to me for anything. The room at the end of the hall is yours." Honey stormed back into the bedroom and slammed the door.

Cherry stood in shock. She missed Destiny. The nights sounded as if they were pretty much the same here. At least during the day she and Destiny had talked and built some form of a friendship. Cherry wasn't sure what to do. She walked around the apartment. Two stained towels hung on the towel rack in the bathroom. Piles of makeup covered the counter. The back bedroom contained a bed and nothing else. A single light bulb dangled from the ceiling. The windows were boarded up, so there was no hope of light or escape.

Cherry made her way to the kitchen as her stomach started to growl. She opened the cabinets. She found a jar of peanut butter, a box of stale cereal, and three bottles of pills. She popped open one of the lids. Just like the ones Destiny had given her every day. At least that would be familiar. If nothing else, Cherry could count on the drugs to get her through.

A few hours later Cherry woke up on the couch to the sound of a hair dryer. Honey was up and getting ready. The clock on the stove read five o'clock. She had one hour to get ready. She heard footsteps and there stood Honey looking back at her.

"Do you know how to do your own makeup?"

"Yeah," Cherry said, walking to the closet in the hall.

"Well, get dressed and get to it. I'm not gonna face T's wrath 'cause you ain't ready."

Cherry began sorting through the dresses. Even if the place was foreign to her, she knew what T expected.

CHAPTER 26

"Ms. Ellis, it's Detective Johnson."

"Good morning. Are you calling with good news?"

"Ma'am, I just received a phone call from a woman who saw the flyer at the library. She used to see Hope on MARTA a few times a week. She remembers Hope talking to a young African American male. They sat together and talked several times. We've asked her to come down to the station and meet with our sketch artist. Maybe we can figure out what this guy looks like."

"Oh, Detective Johnson, that is good news. Thank you!"

"I believe it's our first tip as a result of the flyer Hope's friends put out."

*   *   *

Sydney couldn't believe the turn out for youth group. Word must have gotten out about Hope. They all prayed first, then lots of ideas were thrown out about which ministry to choose to help. When Jeremy, one of the oldest youth members, spoke, everyone listened.

"It's called Hope Ministries. How cool is that? Her name is in the title and everything. They do events downtown in Centennial Park once a month to reach out to the homeless, drug addicts, and prostitutes. We'd all have to go through an all-day training seminar on a Saturday in order to volunteer, but they can use just about anybody, even if you think you have nothing to offer." Jeremy passed out information sheets. "They need worship leaders, prayer warriors, cooks, runners, greeters, set up and break down, and even people in the medical field. I looked at some other places but kept coming back to this because of the name."

"It's perfect!" Sydney squealed. "We'll have the chance to offer hope to others while we're searching for Hope."

Everyone agreed. They decided to sign up for the training seminar. The youth group leader stood up to dismiss the group. "Everyone talk with your parents about this tonight. Take them to the website and make sure they're cool with you doing this, then go online and sign up for the training day. We'll meet at the church at eight o'clock Saturday morning and ride together. Don't forget to bring a release form. You can find it on the church website."

"Yeah, Jeremy, this is awesome! I can't wait to call Ms. Ellis tonight and tell her about it." Sydney hugged him.

*　*　*

Not a night went by that Sydney didn't pray for her childhood friend. Hope had been missing for months, but Sydney could feel in her gut that Hope was still alive. She couldn't just sit by and do nothing. Maybe her prayers would help. Until then, she would love those who crossed her path as part of Hope Ministries. And she would encourage others to do the same.

The whole youth group, as well as several families from church, went through the volunteer training at Hope Ministries.

Sydney could hardly contain her excitement for their first day in the field. The worship leader, Sam, had asked her to join him in leading worship. She was scared for Hope. Sometimes, she'd close her eyes and try to imagine her best friend's face, and it was hard to see her, even though they had grown up together. Being gone abstracted Hope, turned her into a mirage for Sydney. She felt blessed to be volunteering. Even if she couldn't find Hope, she could help people who were maybe a little like her.

Sydney had called Ms. Ellis before they left and told her what they were doing. Even though Ms. Ellis tried to hide it, Sydney knew she was crying.

"I want to be a part of it. I just can't this month. My boss is making me work late again. But I will be there as often as I can."

"I'll call you later this weekend and let you know how it goes."

"Thank you, Sydney. I know you're doing this for Hope. She may never know about it, but I do, and you have no idea what this means to me. I love you. Be safe."

Sydney was about to have her voice blasted across downtown Atlanta for the first time. She and Hope had been to Centennial Park several times when they were little; if only life had stayed that simple.

Sydney said a prayer and took a deep breath before she took the stage.

She looked out over the crowd and saw her mom standing behind the food table. Hannah gave Sydney two thumbs up.

* * *

It had been months since Cherry had moved in with Honey, or at least Cherry thought it had been months. It was hard to keep track of time when one day blurred into the next. There were no events to mark time. Every day was the same: wake up, clean the apartment, eat whatever T brought by, get ready to party. She worked all night until she physically couldn't move, then passed out until the next day came to do it all over again.

She thought it would be better to die than to live in the hell she was in, but T didn't leave enough drugs in the apartment to let it happen. She knew because at one point she'd taken all the pills she could find; all she managed to do was make herself sick for a few days. She paid for it by having to work the day shift and the night shift with only a couple of hours sleep; T told her she had to make up the money he lost when she was sick. There was no escape. Even death was out of her reach.

T came by and told them to be ready early tonight because he wanted to take some pictures. He'd heard the pimps in Vegas were marketing their girls with photos and decided he would give it a try. With baseball season starting, he wanted to be ready to market Sugar Land, as he called it. Cherry couldn't imagine how they could possibly service more customers, but she knew if there were a way to do it, T would figure it out.

She and Honey developed a pattern of coexisting, even though Honey actively disliked Cherry. They were both ready and waiting for T to come by for pictures. Maybe Honey would talk to her. What did she have to lose? She knocked on Honey's door.

"What?" Honey didn't bother to open the door.

"Can I talk to you for a minute?" Cherry cracked the door.

"Isn't that what you're doing?"

Cherry walked in the room, Honey never looked up from her pillow.

"Have I done something to make you mad? You haven't said more than ten words to me since I moved in here. I don't want to be here any more than you want me here. Why are you pissed at me?"

"You haven't figured it out, have you?" Honey stood up and glared at Cherry.

"If I figured it out, I wouldn't be asking." Cherry rolled her eyes.

"It doesn't pay to care in this world. Every time I've ever cared for anyone it came back to bite me. First my parents, then T. I tried again with the last girl who lived here. We became friends." Honey sat down and hugged her pillow.

"We were brought to the ranch about the same time and we were scared to death. She was a little older than me; she looked out for me. She was the closest thing to a friend I ever had and then she turned on me too. She went to T and asked what she had to do to get out of here. She told him she'd sell her soul to the devil if she had to, but she had to be able to see the outside. He normally made his girls put in more time than she had before he let them work on the outside, but she begged him. So she got out of hell and left me behind. But it cost her." Honey looked away.

"What do you mean, it cost her?"

Honey's head snapped back to Cherry's as if she'd been slapped. "She's dead. She got pregnant and now she's dead. T said a john went crazy on her after she'd turned a trick, and by the time he got there he couldn't do anything to save her, but I'll never believe it. She told me he was taking her to get an abortion. She never came back. The only friend I had. I can't let anyone else in. The price is too high. So don't take it personal. It has nothing to do with you. I'm sure you're sweet and all, but I just can't risk it again." Honey fell back on her bed and rolled over, turning away from Cherry.

Cherry sat next to Honey and tentatively reached out to touch her, but thought better of it.

"Honey, I'm sorry about your friend."

The apartment door burst open. "Hey, hey, ladies. It's picture time. Are you ready?" T sounded like it was Christmas morning and the Schwinn bike he wanted was under the tree.

"Yeah, we're coming." Cherry walked out of the room so Honey would have a minute to get herself together.

CHAPTER 27

"We're going big time, ladies. For the first time ever we're pulling the herd out of the stables and taking a group picture." Excitement danced in T's eyes as he unveiled his plan.

"The Braves are expected to have an incredible year. Broadcasters predict they could have sellout crowds at every game. We don't want to miss an opportunity, so we're going to do a little marketing and let the gentlemen of Atlanta know Sweet T has the best sugar in the city." He licked his lips. Cherry's stomach turned.

The girls followed him out the door. He led them into the back of a U-Haul truck where there were close to twenty girls waiting with Slick Rick. Cherry looked around the group in shock. There were blondes, brunettes, redheads, black, white, Asian—T had his own version of the United Nations. No longer did she have to wonder how many girls lived in the apartment complex. But now she wondered how many girls had come before her and were no more? Was Honey's friend the only girl who had died, or were there others? Just the thought of it sent a shiver down her spine.

"Everybody grab a seat. We're going for a little photo shoot, and if you do a good job, then Daddy's gonna feed you a nice dinner before we go to work tonight." T closed the back of the truck after the last girl climbed in.

A single lounge chair was set up in the back of the truck, so most of the girls were forced to sit on the cold metal floor. They sat in the dark and didn't make a sound. Finally, Cherry couldn't take it any longer.

"My name is Cherry, or at least that's what they call me now. It doesn't matter what my name used to be. That girl died a few months ago."

The silence that followed hurt her ears. Finally someone else spoke.

"My name is Sassy. I just got here a few days ago. Will we ever get out of here?" The girl sniffled. Cherry thought she might be crying.

"Baby girl, no one ever escapes from hell." It took a moment for Cherry to recognize Honey's voice.

One by one the girls identified themselves by their street names and told approximately how long they'd been there. Some had been in captivity for years, some for weeks, and others had no idea how long they'd been locked up. As the truck came to a stop, they got quiet again. Cherry knew if T caught them talking with one another, he would punish them.

When T opened the back of the truck, they walked out single file like cattle going to slaughter. They were in an empty warehouse. Cherry had hoped to be outside for a little fresh air, but it must have been too risky. A photographer had set up a backdrop with a white sheet. Rick grabbed the lounge chair out of the back of the U-Haul while T shook hands with the photographer and talked for a few minutes.

"Okay, ladies, this here is Hector. Do exactly what he says and don't ask questions. Time is money, and if you cost me extra money now, you'll earn it back for me plus interest." T slapped Hector on the back. "They're all yours."

Hector worked quickly with few words. Cherry could tell he was nervous around T; however, he took his time looking over each girl as he placed her for photos. Rick stood close by, watching every move. Within minutes Hector began shooting. First he took pictures of each girl separately. Next he brought the lounge chair onto the set and called T over. T removed his shirt and took his position on the lounge chair. Hector placed the girls around T in all sorts of provocative poses; there would be no question what kind of business Sugar Land was. He took a variety of shots, adjusted the poses and snapped a few more before looking at T and nodding. T stood up and put his shirt back on.

"Okay, ladies. I think I promised you a nice dinner."

He waved to Rick and he opened the door to the warehouse. Another truck pulled in. A man Cherry had never seen got out of the truck.

"Where do you want me to set this up?" The man looked at the girls like he hadn't seen a female in years.

"There is good." T pointed to the left of the U-Haul truck.

The man began setting up tables and a buffet of food. It smelled like heaven. Cherry's mouth watered. She hadn't had hot food in longer than she could remember. Her diet had consisted of cereal and occasionally a sandwich or cold pizza. The girls knew better than to say a word or make a move. They kept their eyes down and waited for T's instructions. Once everything was in place, the man looked to T and nodded.

He waved to all the girls in the room. "Your pick."

The man walked up and down the line, looking at each girl in detail as if he were purchasing a car; then he reached for the youngest girl. He took her by the hand and led her to the back of his truck. The photographer chose next. T nodded his head toward the U-Haul and the man led the girl to the back door. Tears swam in her eyes, but she knew better than to say a word. The man stepped up into the truck and pulled the girl up to join him. He looked back to the group, grinning before he closed the door.

Everyone was afraid to move. They knew the food was intended to be a treat for them; however, it would be hard to enjoy it, knowing what it cost.

"Don't let things get cold, girls. We gotta be outta here soon. Eat!" T picked up a plate, and he and Rick served themselves first.

Cherry looked at Honey, who cast her eyes down. Cherry followed her lead; she didn't want to give T a reason to offer her as dessert. She picked up a plate and moved mechanically down the table. She'd lost her appetite, but she knew she would have to force it down. T expected them to eat and be grateful.

Once everyone had finished eating, T banged on the back of the trucks. In a few moments, the doors opened and the men hopped out. One was wiping his mouth as he did. The caterer tucked his shirt in as he walked over to the buffet table and began packing things up. The young girl climbed out of the back of his truck with a tear-streaked face. The other girl was in the back corner of the U-Haul getting dressed. Cherry wanted to go to them, especially the young girl, but she knew it would only bring trouble on them all. Each girl quietly filed back into the truck.

"What? Don't Daddy get a thank you for providing you with a nice dinner tonight?"

"Thank you, Daddy," they said collectively.

"Sassy, you and Candy will get your dinner when we get back to the ranch. Thanks for picking up the tab." He chuckled at his sick joke as he closed the door.

The ride to the apartments was quiet, except for the occasional sniffling. Just when Cherry thought it couldn't get any worse, things like this happened. Maybe Honey was right. Maybe it was best not to care about anyone; then there was no room for more pain.

When they arrived back at the apartment complex Rick took care of lockup. Honey and Cherry were heading to their apartment when T stopped them.

"Cherry, Honey, I need to see you." The girls turned to face him. Cherry told herself to stay calm as her anxiety started to build.

"I've got a special job for you tonight. There's a man in town for a short visit. He asked for my best girls to entertain him and his business partner. I'm giving you the chance to prove you're my best girls. Rick will stay here and manage the ranch, and I'll be driving the two of you to a hotel. You'll enter the hotel from the back door; I have a key for you. You go to his room, do whatever he asks and come back out the same door. You've both done a job like this before with Destiny, so you know the drill. If you do a good job, you can have the rest of the night off. If you mess it up, you'll wish you didn't." He looked at them sternly. "Now go change into the outfits on your beds. Apparently this guy likes cheerleaders."

The girls found cheerleading uniforms in their rooms—including pom-poms. The skirts were super short with no briefs to go under the skirts. Once they were both dressed, they went to the bathroom to remove the heavy makeup they'd put on for the photo shoot.

"You think we should do ponytails?" Cherry looked in the mirror at her shorter layers.

"It couldn't hurt, but how are you going to make it work?" Honey had her golden locks in a ponytail in two seconds.

"I'll just pull the sides up and do half up half down." Cherry reached for the barrettes.

"Let me guess, you were a cheerleader in a former life."

"No, but I was friends with some of the cheerleaders in middle school."

Cherry and Honey worked quickly fixing their hair and makeup. They looked like they were on their way to a football game.

"Not bad." T walked around them checking out both sides. "Not bad at all. We can't have you walking through the hotel with your asses hanging out, so put these on." He handed them each a long raincoat.

T drove to a hotel in the heart of the city. Turning the car off, he turned to them in the backseat.

"Now don't be stupid. You know what will happen to you if you do anything other than what I've told you." His eyes locked on Honey.

They nodded at him, pulled their coats tight around their bodies, and headed toward the back door of the hotel.

"Do you hear that?" Cherry referred to the faint sound of music in the distance.

"Probably just something going on in the park. Let's go, we don't want to make T mad."

Cherry couldn't shake the sound of the music as she rode up in the elevator. Something about it sounded familiar. Just then the elevator door opened. She didn't have time to worry about music. She had a job to do.

"Showtime." Honey stepped out of the elevator waving the room key in her hand. "Don't mess this up. I want the night off."

Cherry nodded. She had survived this before. It couldn't be worse. They knocked on the door.

"Come in," they heard a man call.

When they opened the door, they found two men sitting at a table. They had charts, computers, and papers all over the table. It looked like an office or something.

"Look, Larry," one of the men said, "I told you cheerleaders liked geeks better than jocks. Let me take your coats." He seemed almost giddy. He hung their coats up and came back to give the girls his full attention.

"How about a cheer?"

* * *

"Those guys were freaks!" Honey stepped back into the elevator.

"Yeah, well, those freaks just got us the rest of the night off." Cherry held up a wad of cash. "My friend Larry said we were amazing, and he gave us a hundred-dollar tip."

Cherry couldn't remember the last time she'd gone to bed before sunrise. When they got back to the apartment, they found a hot pizza and a case of beer waiting.

"You girls keep getting tips like this, and you'll become my new downtown girls. Might even get to spend a few nights in the city." T whistled as he closed the door and locked it.

Cherry and Honey sat on the floor in their cheerleading uniforms eating pizza and drinking beer. After she had eaten her fill, Cherry took a long, hot shower and crawled into bed. She looked forward to sleep, but it didn't come. Her mind kept going back to the familiar sound she heard as they walked into the hotel. Where had she heard that song before? Eventually, the drugs kicked in and she fell fast asleep.

CHAPTER 28

Amanda's days were empty and robotic as the months ticked by. Wake up, go to work, come home, go to bed. The loneliness was unbearable.

"Hello?"

"Hey, Ms. Ellis, this is Detective Johnson." Her daughter had been missing almost a year.

Maybe today would be the day he had news about Hope.

"Oh, hi, detective. How have you been?"

"I may have news. I'm almost there, so I'll see you in a few minutes."

Amanda tried not to get her hopes up. Many of the leads Detective Johnson followed up on hadn't panned out. She prayed he wouldn't give up. As she flipped the switch on the coffeepot, the phone rang again.

"Hello."

"Hey, Ms. Ellis. It's Sydney. How are you?"

"Oh, hi, Sydney. I'm fine. More importantly, how are you? I thought about you all night last night." Amanda pulled two coffee mugs out of the cabinet, then grabbed cream and sugar.

"I'm great. We had such an amazing time. I could hardly wait to call and tell you all about it."

"Honey, I'm proud of you. Listen, someone's at my door, can I call you back?"

"Sure, or better yet, you can join us for dinner. Daddy is going to grill out, and we thought it would be nice to have you join us."

"Thanks, that's sweet. I'll call your mom later to find out what I can bring. I hate to run, but I need to get the door. See you tonight."

"Bye, Ms. Ellis."

Detective Johnson walked in. Amanda placed a cup of hot coffee in front of him.

"Well, first of all, our lead from the flyer finally came to the station to meet with our sketch artist. I don't know why she couldn't come in sooner. But it's been so long, we didn't really get anywhere. She wasn't able to give us any distinctive features to separate him from hundreds of other tall, black men in their twenties."

He sipped his coffee to let things sink in before continuing.

"She said he wore a cap that covered his face and he always slouched down in his seat, so she didn't get a good look at him. I'm sorry. I know you were hoping we'd find out more from her."

"Was Hope with the same guy each time the woman saw her?"

"She only remembered seeing them twice, but she was certain it was the same guy both times. She said the second time she saw them they were obviously together."

Amanda gazed out the back window with a puzzled expression on her face. "That's so strange. Hope never mentioned anything to me about meeting anyone on the train."

"She might have been afraid you would make her quit volunteering at the library on MARTA days, especially since this guy was older than her. You might have prevented her from spending time with him."

"What makes you think he was more than a mere acquaintance?"

"That's the second thing I wanted to tell you. I went back through Hope's journal just to make sure we didn't miss something the first time around and I'm glad I did. We thought the last entry was about her drug use, but there was more."

He sat his coffee down and looked at her. "She had skipped to the back half of her journal and started writing again. This time she wrote about a guy called T. We don't know if he went by T or if she just used the letter T to represent his name so no one would know who she was talking about. Either way, it sounds like this guy T was the man from MARTA. She talks about how she could tell him anything and he always understood. She said he was always there and didn't make commitments he didn't keep."

Amanda hung her head. "She's talking about me." Amanda shook her head. Then a look of recognition crossed her face. "Do you think T is Troy, the mover?"

"Not likely. Whoever T is, we believe Hope trusted him enough to leave school with him. If Troy raped her, which is what her journal implies, she would do everything she could to avoid him."

Amanda nodded, barely containing her tears.

"But listen, don't beat yourself up. T, whoever that is, saw an opportunity and took it. He played on Hope's vulnerability and naivete. She wrote about how she skipped out of the library early one day to meet him because he wanted to take her out for ice cream to celebrate her project. She also wrote about plans to skip school and meet up with him for the day. That was her last entry."

"So the whole reason she kept asking me if the clothes she tried on at the mall made her look older was because she wanted to look older for him." Amanda was afraid to voice what she already knew.

"Ms. Ellis, we believe T was grooming Hope. We believe she is being trafficked." Amanda saw the pain in Detective Johnson's eyes. He wasn't enjoying his job.

"This guy T went by the book, so to speak. He probably rode MARTA looking for young girls. I'm guessing when he found Hope, he struck up a conversation and left it at that for a few days until she felt comfortable sharing information with him. When these guys learn there's no dad in sight or there is trouble of any kind at home, they move in for the kill. They come across as the understanding friend-turned-boyfriend. Before long, they have the girls eating out of their hands and trusting them. Then it's too late."

"Hope knows better than to talk to strangers." Amanda couldn't stand still. It was more than she could take.

"That's just it, Ms. Ellis. If this guy played it like I think he did, she was talking to him before she even realized it. Once she did, he didn't seem like a stranger anymore."

"So you're saying my daughter is a prostitute?" Amanda tried to fix herself another cup of coffee but ended up pouring until it overflowed all over the counter. She wiped it up and started pacing again, leaving her cup on the counter.

"Not by choice, Ms. Ellis. Sex trafficking of minors is one of the fastest-growing crimes in Atlanta—actually, in our world. It's been estimated that three hundred thousand children are at risk of being trafficked every year in our country. Atlanta is one of the top cities in the nation. The numbers are staggering. The studies we have available estimate over seven thousand transactions take place a month in Atlanta alone."

Amanda fought to get her mind around what he was saying. "I don't understand. I thought this type of thing took place in third-world countries."

"It happens all over the world, even in America. Even in Atlanta. It's hard to get a handle on, because these guys are smart and they don't leave many trails behind. They keep minors locked away somewhere, so we don't see them out on the streets very often like adult prostitutes. With today's technology, pimps use the Internet and cell phones to advertise girls. The johns, the guys who pay for sex with minors, go to the girls, instead of the other way around. It's hard to catch them, but we're not giving up."

"Oh, dear God, please keep my baby safe!" Amanda's legs gave way and she collapsed in a chair as Hope's reality sank in.

She excused herself from the kitchen and practically ran to her bedroom in the back of the house. She needed to scream. She wanted to hit something. She grabbed a pillow from her bed and screamed into it until she was spent. She blew her nose and washed her face to regain her composure.

Walking back into the kitchen, she found Detective Johnson waiting patiently for her. She warmed her coffee in the microwave and sat down again at the kitchen table.

"Is this why the other officers brought you in on the case? Did they suspect this all along?"

"Honestly, Ms. Ellis, they weren't sure. They didn't know where else to turn, so they figured it wouldn't hurt to bring me in. I tend to look at things differently than other officers because of my experience with cases like this."

"What are the chances I'll ever see my daughter again?" She looked away, not wanting to voice her next question. "Is she even alive?"

"Chances are good Hope is alive. If she is being trafficked, her pimp sees her as money, so he won't hurt her unless he feels he has to. He can't very well market a girl who is bruised or in a cast. As far as seeing her again, we can only hope. We've rescued ten girls in the last year. We've learned a lot about how the pimps in this area operate from the girls we've rescued. We put undercover officers in the field whenever we have a tip of young girls being seen with older men. Some even pose as johns from time to time, so they can get information we need to collapse these rings."

"How long will you look for her?"

"You have my word I will do everything in my power to find Hope."

"Thank you, detective. I don't know how you do what you do day in and day out, but I am thankful for you." She reached over and squeezed his hand. With as much time as he had spent at her house, she was beginning to think of him as a friend instead of a police officer doing his job.

"Can I call Mrs. Clarkston for you? I don't think you should be alone right now."

"No, thank you. I just need to process everything. I'm supposed to go to her house in a little while anyway, so I won't be alone. Thank you for everything, even though I'm more worried now. I'm starting to feel like you're my friend."

"That goes two ways, Ms. Ellis." Detective Johnson said, as a sad smile entered his eyes. "If you think you'll be okay, I'm going to let you get back to your day." He stood to go.

She walked him to the door. Amanda was moved by his dedication to Hope's case. "Thank you, Detective Johnson. I'm so grateful."

After he left, Amanda curled up on the sofa and hugged a pillow close to her chest. Tears flowed. Hard, choking tears. What kind of animal does that to a child? She is a child. She's only fourteen. Then she remembered—Hope turned fifteen. But she wasn't home to celebrate. Amanda fell to the floor, her body heaving tears.

* * *

Amanda jolted awake. She looked at the clock. It was six, and she hadn't called Hannah back. She must have cried herself to sleep. As she reached for the phone it rang.

"Hello?"

"Amanda, is everything all right?" Hannah sounded alarmed. "Sydney said she called and you were busy but said you'd call back. We got worried when we didn't hear from you."

"I'm sorry." She didn't know where to begin.

"What are you not telling me, Amanda? Have you heard something about Hope?"

Amanda stifled a sob. "Detective Johnson came by today. He said the woman who identified Hope from the picture on MARTA couldn't give them a decent description of the guy she saw her with. All they know is he is an African American male in his twenties."

"Oh, Amanda, I know you were hoping she would lead us to Hope."

"That's not all. He was rereading her journal to see if he missed anything and found she had skipped some pages and started writing about a guy she met on MARTA. She called him T. They think she's being trafficked."

Amanda looked at her phone to make sure they were still connected, "I don't know what to say. How can . . ."

"Oh, Hannah, what kind of hell is my baby girl living through right now?" Her sobs escaped. "She's got to be so scared. I want to help her, but . . . What am I going to do?" She could barely catch her breath between sobs.

"I'm coming to get you. The last thing you need is to be alone right now. Why don't you pack a bag and just plan on staying the night with us?"

"I appreciate it, Hannah, but I think I'm gonna stay here."

"Forward your calls to your cell phone. You've done it before. I'm not taking no for an answer. I'll be there in thirty minutes."

Amanda was dressed and ready with an overnight bag when Hannah pulled into the driveway. As Amanda walked outside, Sydney jumped out of the car and threw her arms around her. Sydney's eyes were red from crying. They clung to each other without saying a word. They needed each other. Finally, Sydney pulled back, wiping her eyes.

"Daddy's making steak and shrimp for us on the grill. It should be good." She tried so hard to sound upbeat. "Mom and I want to tell you and Daddy about our time with Hope Ministries last night. Every month gets better and better."

"I'd like that." Amanda climbed in the car, and noticed the leaves were starting to fall. Months . . . it had been months since Hope went missing. Would she ever see her daughter again?

CHAPTER 29

Amanda's legs burned as she pounded out her frustration on the pavement. She finished up her Saturday morning run and thought about another month of missing Hope Ministries because of working late. Another Saturday morning of feeling left out. She hated only volunteering once every few months. She grabbed her phone and dialed Hannah's number as she walked in the house.

"Hey, Hannah. How did it go last night?"

"Incredible."

"I hate that I wasn't able to be there. Call me crazy, but being down there with the drug addicts and prostitutes makes me feel closer to my daughter."

"I can see that. I think we all feel that. Oh, by the way, I saw your buddy Carlos. He came down to let us know he found a job and has been clean for three weeks."

"I hate I missed him. That young man has such potential. All he needs is someone to believe in him."

"He said as much last night. He told me you reminded him of his mom and when you told him you believed he could get clean it was like hearing it from her."

"Well, if I can't help Hope, I want to help whoever I can. Maybe someone will come along and help her find her way back home."

"I believe it, Amanda." Hannah paused. "Hey, listen, I'm calling about Thanksgiving. I'd love to have you join us."

"I know better than to argue with you, so just tell me what to bring."

It had taken Amanda a long time to stop feeling like the Clarkston's charity case. The Clarkston family had become more than just friends in this last year. They had become her family.

"I was thinking of asking Detective Johnson and his wife, Laura, to join us too. Do you think they would come?"

"Hannah, that's a wonderful idea! I think it would mean a lot to them."

"Great! I've gotta run, but I wanted to get my guest list firmed up so I could start planning the meal. It will be here soon!"

"Have a great day!" Amanda couldn't believe Hope would be spending her second Thanksgiving away from home. Amanda wondered if she'd ever spend another holiday with her daughter. She wasn't looking forward to the holidays. Maybe they'd be easier this year. She struggled to put one foot in front of another amid all the joyful people. She went about her day-to-day activities without tears, but the constant pain remained. Where was her baby? What was she doing? Would she come home if she could? Was she choosing not to?

The questions would overtake her if she let them. Instead, she decided to go shopping. She didn't have a lot of money, but she wanted to buy one or two small gifts for the Clarkston family for Christmas. After all they'd done for her and Hope, it was the least she could do.

CHAPTER 30

From the chill in the air and decorations in the city, Cherry decided it must be close to Christmas, but she had no idea of the date. It didn't matter, anyway. T never gave them a day off. Christmas was just another day in hell. At least she and Honey got outside to breathe fresh air. They went with T downtown several times a month.

The two girls were friends, though Honey had tried to fight it. They lived together and were the only ones allowed off the ranch to work what T called "destination jobs." He typically required the johns to come to the ranch because he had more control. But with the Falcons playing well and drawing big crowds in the city, he wasn't about to miss an opportunity.

Some weeks Honey and Cherry would stay in the city multiple nights in order to service all the clients. When that happened, T would take them to an apartment to sleep. Cherry didn't know if it was his apartment or someone else's. She didn't care. She got to take a hot shower, eat real food, and sleep in a comfortable bed for the night. Those luxuries were hard to come by, and she was grateful.

"Get up, girl. We gotta get you something new to wear for tonight." T stood at the foot of her bed. She knew better than to keep him waiting. She crawled out of bed and followed him into the living room.

"Do I have time to take a shower?" She tried to stifle a yawn.

"Yeah, but be quick. Time is money." He didn't look up from his phone. He was busy texting someone. Most likely he was sending pictures to a new client.

Cherry showered and was dressed in no time. She knew it would only take one mistake to send her back to the ranch.

"Where's Honey?" Cherry couldn't believe she asked T a question. She braced herself for a punch, but he was so engrossed in his texting that he didn't catch it.

"She back at the ranch. Tonight's a solo job, and Daddy's gonna see if you can handle it." He put his phone away.

"I can handle it!" she said with attitude.

"That's my girl. That's why I'm taking you out. You do what your Daddy say and you don't give me no trouble." He ran a hand down her cheek, looking her straight in the eye.

"By the way, I rode by your house to check on Mama. She don't look like she's missing you none. It's a good thing you got me to take care of you, girl. You know Daddy loves you, right? You know I look out for you." He drew her close to him, daring her to disagree.

Could her mom have really moved on? Is it possible that she didn't miss her? Cherry wanted to believe T was lying, but she couldn't be sure.

"Maybe after we get your dress we'll have time for Daddy to show you how much he loves you, baby girl." He claimed her mouth in a hungry kiss as his hands roamed up and down her body.

Cherry didn't want to respond to him, but she knew better than to hold back. She kissed him until he broke away.

Cherry hadn't been shopping since she moved to the ranch. She had no idea where they would go. She just wanted to spend the day out. She couldn't picture T shopping the whole day with her. T stopped to get gas and the back door opened. Cherry turned to see Destiny climb in the backseat.

"Hey, girl, what up?" Destiny gave Cherry a hug.

"What are you doing here?" Cherry screamed with excitement. It seemed like forever since she'd seen Destiny.

"T ain't gonna do no shopping, girl. You ought to know that," Destiny said, "and he don't trust you enough to let you go on your own yet. I'm taking you. He'll drop us off and come get us. You must be doing good if he picked you for this job. It used to be mine before I started grooming."

"What's the job?" The front car door opened. They both knew better than to discuss things in front of T. Destiny shot Cherry a sharp look and shook her head. Cherry let the matter drop. She would wait until they were alone.

T dropped them off at a shopping center and told them they had two hours to get nails done and a dress purchased. He handed a wad of cash to Destiny.

"Get yourself something too, girl." He squeezed Destiny's butt. "Maybe I'll let you ride with me tonight and while she's working we can have our own little party." He licked his lips.

Cherry found herself sitting in the same nail salon T had taken her to the first time she'd had her nails done. She and Destiny didn't say much while in the store. Too many ears around. Cherry sat back and closed her eyes, soaking in the gentle touch of the technician. They left the nail salon and took off to find a dress. She wanted to get something red, but Destiny told her it wouldn't look good with her red hair.

"Can we color my hair jet black? We have time?" Cherry poked out her bottom lip trying to pout, but she was fighting a laugh.

"Look girl, we got time, but T might not like it." Destiny seemed indecisive.

"But I want the red dress, for Christmas. You color my hair and I'll convince T he likes it."

Destiny laughed. "What you know about Christmas?"

"I saw Christmas decorations up the last time I was out. I know what Christmas looks like. Please, Destiny, can't you call him and ask him?"

Destiny hung up the phone and turned to Cherry smiling.

"Okay, girl, go try on the red dress but it better look hot or else I'm not coloring your hair. You look like you need a trim too, while I'm at it." Destiny ran her hands through Cherry's hair.

Cherry found a red dress that sparkled with electricity it had so much glitter on it. She grabbed some black platform heels to match. When she came out of the dressing room, Destiny grinned.

"Okay, Cinderella, let's jump. If I gotta get your hair colored too, we ain't got time to waste having a fashion show." Cherry squealed. Rarely did anything go her way. Being able to make one simple choice was a major victory.

Destiny must have been feeling a little festive too, because she bought a green dress. After paying for the dresses, they were off to the drugstore to buy hair color, then to the house to color Cherry's hair.

Being able to walk to the house talking like two normal girls made Cherry feel like a bird out of a cage.

"Does anyone live at the house with you?"

Destiny wouldn't make eye contact with her. "No, Sassy was the last one. T has one he's watching, but she ain't bit the hook yet. He'll reel her in. He always does."

It didn't take long before Cherry had a head full of jet-black hair.

"Let me trim up around your face a bit." Destiny pulled out her scissors.

When she finished with the ends, she stepped back to get a better look. "Damn, you're pretty!" Destiny shook her head. "T's gonna be happy with you, girl. Play your cards right and you might get out of that hellhole he locks you in for good."

"What do you mean?" Cherry looked in the mirror, playing with her new hairdo.

Destiny looked over her shoulder to make sure no one was coming up the sidewalk. "I heard him and Rick talking one night about how they need to keep a girl or two in the city so they don't have to keep running 'em when the big deals go down. They want someone living there to send out. T said he'd have to trust her not to run. They don't know I heard 'em talking. They thought I was asleep. I think tonight is a test for you, so do it right, girl. You're too special to be locked up at the ranch like an animal."

Cherry had forgotten how much she enjoyed Destiny's company.

"T's always looking for a way to make money faster, isn't he?" She ran her hand through her new hair one last time before putting the mirror away.

Destiny said nothing and started cleaning up the hair on the floor.

"Get your dress and makeup on. He'll be here soon. He's bringing food."

By the time Cherry finished her makeup, she heard T in the kitchen talking with Destiny. He sounded like he was in a good mood.

When Cherry walked into the room he stopped eating. "Damn girl, you looking hot! Gonna make me some big money tonight! Set your ass down and eat something, because you gonna be busy tonight. Destiny, be ready by the time she's done, because we can't keep the man waiting."

"Where are we going?" Cherry forgot for a moment who she was talking to.

T slapped her across the face so hard her food flew out of her mouth. She sat there stunned. She knew better than to ask T questions. It was against the rules. She got up and cleaned up the mess on the floor before settling back down to eat.

"Girl, I hate hurting you. Why you make me hurt you?" T kept eating.

Cherry responded without looking up. "I'm sorry, T. I'm sorry I asked you a question."

Before long they were all in the car riding into the city. Cherry enjoyed looking at the Christmas lights. She always loved Christmas. But she had to stop thinking about it. Life was different now.

"Okay, girl, we're going to a condo complex. You knock on the door, and if someone asks who it is, you tell them special delivery. The man asked for you for the night, so I'll be back early to pick you up. He's paying big for this, so you give him what he paid for and I'll be a happy man. If I'm happy, then you're happy. Don't mess up. Got it?" T gave her a warning look as he patted her face.

"I won't mess up, T. I can do this."

No matter what she had to do tonight, she would do it in order to get off the ranch and into the apartment in town. While it was just geography, at least she would have fresh air and sunshine in the city. If Destiny was right, this was her ticket out.

Cherry knocked on the door and a man in a suit answered. He looked her up and down and then broke into a big smile.

"Oh, look, my Christmas present has arrived. Right on time."

He took her hand and twirled her around like a ballerina, admiring every inch of her. He drew her into the condominium. "Merry Christmas to me." He laughed at his own joke as he closed the door.

*　*　*

T picked Cherry up as the sun was coming up. She handed him a wad of hundred dollar bills. She was too tired to count it, but T wasn't. He was never too tired to count money. She climbed in the back seat of the car and crashed. Destiny was nowhere to be found.

"You done good, baby girl. You earned yourself another night in the crib." He drove her back to the apartment in the city.

Cherry climbed into the steaming hot shower. She didn't know if she could handle many more nights like that. She expected to spend the night with one man. She didn't realize he bought her for the night so she could entertain all of his associates. There must have been twenty-five men in the condo. Her body was racked with pain; even her hair hurt. She wanted to go to sleep and never wake up. After nearly scrubbing her skin off in the shower, she climbed into the bed, swallowed two pills, and fell asleep before her head hit the pillow.

CHAPTER 31

After several more jobs in the city, T found Cherry trustworthy and moved her to the city apartment permanently. As she grabbed her things from the ranch, Honey watched her angrily.

"This is why I don't care about nobody, because just when I decide to try again, I get stabbed in the back."

"I didn't stab you in the back. What am I supposed to do, tell T no? You know where that will get me. I'd be dead before you could count to ten."

"I'm just mad because I'm not going with you." Honey's face softened.

"I'll try and put in a good word for you. We were a good team when we did those jobs downtown. Maybe he'll see it would make sense to bring you to the city too."

"Just take care of you. I'll take care of me. I always have, I always will." Honey hugged Cherry good-bye. Who knew if they'd ever see each other again?

*   *   *

Cherry thought she would be able to come and go as she pleased in the city, but she couldn't have been more wrong. She was locked in the apartment in the city just as she was at the ranch. At least there was a stereo and a TV. T made sure there were no computers or phones around. He told her she better not make any noise or draw attention from the neighbors or she'd be back at the ranch. Cherry didn't want to do anything to mess up her situation. She could move from room to room, and the kitchen was stocked with food, real food. She could even go out on the balcony and get fresh air. It wasn't freedom, but it was as close as she would ever come.

Working in the city was just as busy as the ranch, but Cherry went to the johns instead of them coming to her. She would meet them in apartments, corporate condos, and even offices after hours. Always close by, T made sure she played by the rules. Sometimes he would set her up in a hotel room for the night and the johns would come to her one after another. She made a lot of money, but she never saw any of it. She knew better than to hold back from T. That could get a girl killed. Every now and then T would give her money for cigarettes or to get her nails done, but that was it.

"What you need money for, girl? You've got it made living in this place. As long as you take care of me, I'll take care of you."

T treated her well. Sometimes she even believed him when he told her he loved her. One night after work he pulled her into his lap and told her how special she was to him.

"T, I was thinking it might be a good idea to bring Honey to the apartment. She and I made good money together when we did parties. Then I would have more time to spend with you."

T stood up so fast he dropped Cherry to the floor.

"Girl, you just leave the thinking to me. Your job is to make the money, mine is to figure out how. Whenever you start thinking, you get yourself in trouble." He pulled an envelope out of his pocket. "Oh yeah. Thought you might be interested in seeing that your mama is just fine without you."

He tossed pictures of her mom Christmas shopping with Hannah Clarkston in her direction. Her mom actually had a smile on her face. It brought tears to Cherry's eyes. T enjoyed tormenting her with pictures of her mom.

"When did you take these?" Cherry wiped the tears away.

"I took them yesterday while you were working the Christmas party. Your mama look real happy now, don't she? I bet she done forgot you completely."

"Why would you say that? You don't even know her. She would never forget me!" Cherry screamed then covered her mouth. *Oh God, what have I done?*

T grabbed her up by her arm and pulled her inches from his face. His hot breath almost burned her face.

"Listen here, bitch, don't nobody yell at me!" He slapped her so hard she thought he knocked out a tooth.

T started to walk out of the room, but then he turned back. Cherry kept her head down. She didn't want to give him a clear target in case he came back for more.

"If you want her to keep that smile, I suggest you remember your place, whore. I own you. Your body is mine, and you do with it what I tell you to do. You don't tell me how to run my herd. You got it?"

"Yes, sir," she whispered.

"You do that again and you'll find yourself back on the ranch. Maybe Honey would like to hang in the crib with me for a while. I always like me some honey." He licked his lips and rubbed his hands together as if he couldn't wait to get them on her.

Cherry didn't move. It wouldn't take much for her to be replaced. In her mind, going back to the ranch would be death. A prison cell with no daylight, no air.

* * *

Cherry worked hard. T got over his anger and frequently told her how much he loved her. But he really loved the wads of cash she handed him night after night. She began to gain his trust again. A couple of times he set her up in a hotel room and allowed her to walk back to the apartment when she finished for the night. T would leave the door unlocked for her. He didn't trust her with a key. But the freedom of walking down the street alone brought Cherry great pleasure. She would never take it for granted again.

She was always careful to keep her head down and not waste time walking home. The last thing she wanted to do was attract the cops or show up late. T would take away the privilege of walking home if she was late.

She made that mistake once, and he nearly cracked her ribs punching her. Each time he socked her he said, "Girl, you gotta learn!" After the beating, he drew her into his arms.

"Daddy loves you, Cherry. Daddy don't like it when you make me hurt you. Do what Daddy say and he won't have to beat you." Cherry took care not to repeat the things that caused T to become violent.

Cherry came in quietly at sunrise, careful not to disturb T if he was on the phone. She heard voices in the other room but knew better than to look. She put her cash on the desk and went on down the hall to shower. When she turned off the water, she heard a loud knock at the bathroom door.

"Get dressed and come see me."

Why did T want to see her? Had she done something wrong? She'd had a good night. All of her clients seemed pleased. One even gave her a big tip and told her he wanted to see her again. Cherry made her way into the living room, uncertain what awaited her.

"This here is Roxy. She's new to the family. Destiny is a little busy right now, so I brought her here so you can teach her the rules. Can you do that for me, baby?" T reached out to Cherry.

Roxy couldn't have been more than twelve years old. Cherry's stomach knotted. She knew T expected her to speak, but the thought of another innocent girl being dragged into hell made her nauseous.

"You hear me, girl?" T jerked her arm.

"Yes, sir." Cherry smiled at T. "Hey, Roxy, my name is Cherry."

Roxy kept her eyes locked on the floor. Even from where Cherry stood she could see Roxy was trembling.

"Do you want her to share my room?"

"Not tonight." T looked Roxy up and down. "She gonna share my room tonight, right, baby girl? I think I might even have a welcome to the family party for her." He reached out to run his finger down her arm.

Roxy flinched at his touch, and T slapped her hard across the face. Cherry winced on the inside, but she couldn't help Roxy at all by saying anything. Tonight T would teach her what he expected her to do. Then Cherry would show her how he expected her to dress and how to fix her makeup. Cherry remembered how Destiny had been her only source of comfort when T brought her into the herd. She would be that for Roxy.

* * *

Over the next two weeks, Cherry took Roxy with her to every call. Roxy, in her stubbornness, fought the lifestyle and she paid for it with regular beatings from T. Cherry thought he might kill her before he broke her. Eventually, Roxy realized that there was no escape from hell. Cherry tried not to get attached to Roxy, because she knew Roxy was days away from being sent to the ranch.

After Cherry proved successful at training the new girl, T used her whenever Destiny was busy. He seemed to acquire girls left and right. Cherry's stomach turned every time she walked into the apartment and saw someone new. It usually only took a night or two to break them. After a couple of weeks with Cherry, T moved them to the ranch.

One girl haunted Cherry. Her name was Sissy; at least that's what T called her. She fought hard. No matter how badly he beat her, she refused him. One day she was just gone. Cherry hoped he had just moved her out to the ranch early, but she feared the worst. She knew better than to ask about her. Cherry's suspicions were confirmed when T brought a new girl in several weeks later. "Meet Sissy. You teach her what to do, Cherry."

Cherry cried herself to sleep that night. T was the devil. If she'd ever thought she mattered to him, watching new girls come into the herd showed her otherwise. He was smooth and charming to the girls until he got them in the door. Then he turned into someone else and shattered them into a thousand little pieces. He took great pleasure in doing it.

Cherry quickly developed a routine for training girls. She knew T would hold her responsible for whatever the girls did, so she made sure they knew what was expected of them and what would happen to them both if they didn't cooperate.

"You don't have a choice," she repeated Destiny's words. "None of us do."

T began to give her more and more responsibility. He had yet to give her a cell phone like Destiny, but he let her out on her own for some calls. Whenever she had a girl in training, T got them a hotel room close to the apartment, but he was never far away.

T fed Cherry regular pictures of her mother to keep her in line. It was wonderful seeing her mom in pictures, but she knew the real reason T showed her. They were a constant reminder that he was keeping almost as close tabs on her mom as he was on her. Cherry knew T was capable of anything. She would keep her mom safe.

Cherry walked home alone more frequently because T had too many girls to keep up with and Rick wasn't always available to help. T started giving her a little money to buy herself cigarettes or trinkets as a reward for doing well. But freedom? Not even close.

He frequently warned her, "Girl, don't make me sorry I trusted you."

"I won't, T. I know the rules."

During the winter months they worked more hours. From the moment the sun went down they were open for business until the sun came up. T said, "We may doze but we never close"—because if anyone wanted a girl in the middle of the day, T would deliver, whatever it took.

CHAPTER 32

Friday night many volunteers brought extra blankets to give to the people they served. Several of the downtown restaurants donated the use of their outdoor heaters for cold nights. Sydney spent days on the phone talking with restaurant managers and owners explaining Hope Ministries and how they served the community of Atlanta.

"This will be great PR for your company. We'll make sure everyone knows how you support Hope Ministries." Sydney heard "yes" more times than not. She was a natural activist.

She helped set up tables and chairs in the food tent. She prayed for the people who would sit in the seats that evening. Sydney didn't have long before she had to start warming up to lead worship. She got excited just thinking about it.

* * *

"When the bills start rolling in, the men come knocking . . . looking for a stress release. That's why Christmas comes for me in January and February. My favorite time of year." T laughed as his phone started to ring. "See what I mean?"

The workload increased substantially over the holidays. T was thrilled. Cherry hoped that things would be slowing down after New Year's, but T assured her it would be picking up even more. In fact, he told Cherry that she would be on her own for the first part of the night. He needed to go pick up one of the girls at the ranch to help with city traffic. Cherry welcomed the independence.

With a little time to kill, she decided to smoke a cigarette out on the balcony. The cold didn't bother her. She craved the fresh air more than the warmth of the apartment. T came out and handed her a beer and a pill bottle. She swallowed the pills without a word. T pulled her close and ran his hands up and down her sides.

"Damn, girl, you look good. You done real good lately, Cherry. You my best girl, you know that? I don't let nobody else walk. Only you." He kissed her neck.

Cherry was still too shaken by what happened to Sissy to be sucked up in his romance; however, she knew better than to voice her thoughts.

"I got you lined up with a couple of regulars later tonight, but there's a new guy who requested you by name. Word must be getting around about how sweet your sugar is. The dude is at the hotel four blocks down. I can drop you on my way to the ranch, but you'll have to walk back." He lifted her chin so she would have to look him in the eye. "You keep your head down and don't talk to nobody on the outside, you hear me?"

"Yes sir. I won't mess up, T. I know the rules."

"That's my girl." He kissed her again, this time possessively. "We might just have to take us a night here real soon and spend it just me and you. It's been too long, girl. Everybody else been tasting your sugar but me."

"Cause you've been keeping me so busy, T. You may not like sharing, but you don't mind the money." She laughed. The drugs were kicking in and Cherry was feeling bold and in control.

"Look here, girl, I may let others pay for a turn but you belong to me, and don't you ever forget it!" He slammed her up against the sliding glass door and began kissing her neck as he explored her body with his hands. "If we had time, I'd show you," he said, barely above a whisper.

Cherry went to the bathroom to fix her makeup before leaving. T was very strict about looking nice for a job. "Sloppy don't sell," he used to say. T was on the phone with Rick when he escorted Cherry out, leaving the apartment door unlocked behind them. He never allowed her to carry money from one job to the next. So she would need to let herself in to deposit her earnings before going on to her second call.

As T pulled into the hotel parking lot, he turned to Cherry. "Keep Mama safe." He winked at her as she climbed out of the car. Cherry might not be able to save herself, but she would play by the rules and do everything T demanded if it meant her mom would be safe. With that in mind, she snuck past the front desk and made her way up the elevator to the fourth floor. She tapped lightly on the door and only had to wait a second before it opened.

"You're late!" The man was clearly agitated.

Cherry knew that if anything, she was early, but she knew better than to argue with a john.

T always said, "The customer always right. Whatever he says goes. If you make him mad, you make me mad; if you make me mad, you pay for it."

"I'm so sorry, sweetheart. I came as fast as I could." She ran her hand down his chest in a seductive manner. "I'm here now." She forced a smile as the door closed.

* * *

Sydney heard Sam gathering the crew for prayer. "We are here tonight to help the forgotten ones. We're not here to judge; we're here to show these people love. Always work in pairs, and if you get in over your head, come get one of the supervisors or raise your hand and we'll come to you." He looked around the group. "Whatever you do, don't go outside the park. We're here to serve, but we need to be smart and we need to be safe. For anyone new, we have a couple of off-duty police officers who volunteer with us, so if something comes up that makes you uncomfortable, let us know." Sam nodded in Detective Johnson's direction. "We're a team."

Sydney checked her nametag. They were asked to have their Hope Ministries volunteer badge visible at all times so people could get to know one another. It also made it easier to pick out people who wandered into the park.

Sydney looked up as Sam announced, "Okay, gang, something big is going to happen tonight. I don't know what it is, but I've felt it all day as I've prepared. No matter where you're stationed, be alert and ready to do the most good."

Sydney and the other members of Moriah Church circled around to pray again before things kicked off. Anticipation showed on every face.

CHAPTER 33

Back in the Present

She was still for a moment before she realized that she hadn't heard the sequence of locks. She heard T and Rick bound down the hall. She wasn't caged—for the first time in over a year she could open a door and walk outside. She hobbled across the apartment, ignoring the throb of her bruises. There was no time to waste. She cracked the door open and peered down the hallway. It was empty.

With the hood of her sweatshirt drawn over her head, she forced herself to hurry to the stairs, to ignore the pain that seared her body. She couldn't risk the elevator. She reached the door to the stairwell and heard the ding of the elevator. Panicked, she slung the door open. She could only think about surviving.

Cherry reached the ground floor and discovered the lobby was clear. She felt the thumping in her chest slow a bit as she made her way to the back door. She had to get as far away as possible, quickly. Still, she couldn't stop the waves of physical memory of that weasel beating her up. She spat on the sidewalk, tasted metallic blood. She didn't care what she looked like.

She crept from one building to another, looking over her shoulder at every turn, hiding in the darkness. Music played in the distance. It soothed her a bit. As she gave herself a moment to listen, her fear ebbed a bit. She realized that if it weren't for that freak smashing her face up after refusing to pay, she'd probably be under T or some other man. A surge of hope rose in her throat; she took a deep breath and regained a little bit of her energy. "Keep moving," she told herself. Being still anywhere was dangerous. The closer she came to Centennial Park the louder the music got. There was a concert or something. If she could make it to the park, she could get lost in the crowd. Even if T saw her, she would be safe for a while. There would be too many witnesses. She had to get there.

The music stopped. Cherry became a statue. *Please God, no! Don't let it be over.* Where did that come from? She'd given up on prayer a long time ago. Besides, God wouldn't want anything to do with her. She was trash, disposable.

A man's voice pierced her thoughts. *The event wasn't over!* She couldn't make out what he said and she didn't care. She just needed him to keep things going so she could disappear.

She came out from the cover of the buildings and jogged through her pain to the entrance of the park. She looked over her shoulder one last time before slipping into the crowd. As she turned back around, she ran right into something. Or someone. A pair of arms came around her. "God, no!"

"I've got you," a voice said. All color drained from Cherry's face. Would she ever get free? It took her a moment to realize the arms that held her weren't T's. They belonged to a woman. Cherry looked into the softest blue eyes she had ever seen. The woman's face was like the face of an angel, filled with love and compassion.

"Bless your heart. You look like I scared the very life out of you," the woman said. "Let's get you a seat until your color comes back." She led Cherry to a chair inside the park area. "Well now, we need to see about those cuts and bruises on your face." The woman didn't seem the least bit surprised or alarmed by the condition of Cherry's face. What had Cherry stumbled into, and why was this woman so nice to her?

"Sweetheart, this is my friend, Karen. She is going to get you something warm to drink while I tend to those cuts."

The woman named Karen smiled at her. "Would you like coffee or hot chocolate?"

"Hot chocolate, please," Cherry heard herself say. Karen disappeared behind the angel. Before she knew it, Cherry was holding a warm paper cup of hot chocolate. It tasted like a liquid chocolate bar. It warmed her to her toes.

She jerked back to reality. Her eyes darted in all directions. She couldn't sit here in the open, exposed. What if T was near? He would see her instantly.

The woman patted her hand. "My name is Margaret, and you're safe here. We want to help you. Let's get you moved into the medical tent so I can take better care of those cuts." Margaret put her arm around Cherry and walked her toward a white, enclosed tent. Cherry clutched the hot chocolate. The idea of anyone touching her face was unpleasant, but the tent would keep her hidden for a time. She glanced over her shoulder one more time before following the women into the tent. There was no sign of T or Rick.

Margaret quickly cleaned the cuts on her face with antiseptic. It stung, but Cherry didn't flinch. There was something soothing about someone touching her face with such gentleness. It reminded her of her mother's loving touch. She hadn't allowed herself to think about her mother in a while. It only brought her pain.

Margaret spoke quietly to Cherry while she worked. She never asked her name or commented on her cuts, bruises, and swollen eye. She just went about her work with tenderness and care.

"You have the most beautiful brown eyes, dear."

Cherry almost laughed, considering one of her eyes was practically swollen shut. Margaret placed an icepack on Cherry's eye, then led her to another tent for food. Cherry followed obediently.

This was the closest to normal Cherry had felt in a long time. She knew the risk of sitting here long enough to eat a warm meal, but she couldn't make herself leave. She had craved human compassion for so long. Besides, she was hidden from T and Rick as long as she remained in the tent.

Margaret handed her a cup of soup and some bread. The steam soothed Cherry's face. she held the cup for a while before dipping the bread in the soup and taking a tentative bite. Margaret didn't seem to notice. She seemed content to sit beside Cherry while she ate.

"Are you feeling better now that you've eaten something?" Margaret rested her hand on Cherry's shoulder.

"Yes. Do I need to go? Do you need this space for someone else?" Cherry started to stand.

"Heavens, no, you sit here as long as you like. You're safe."

Cherry looked up at Margaret. "Why are you being so nice to me when you don't even know me? You have no idea who I am or what I've done."

"You need help. God tells us whatever we do for someone, we do for Him. By loving you, I'm loving Jesus. Do you know Jesus, sweetheart?"

Those angelic eyes looked at her with such love and compassion, Cherry almost cried. She looked away. It had been a long time since someone had called her sweetheart and meant it as an endearment.

"I used to know Jesus a long time ago. I'm pretty certain He wouldn't want anything to do with me right now. In fact, He'd probably run in the opposite direction."

Just then the man speaking on stage called a young girl to the microphone. The girl seemed to capture Margaret's attention; Cherry followed her gaze. Maybe it was her granddaughter. The girl began to talk about her best friend who lived on the streets.

The swelling had started to go down from her eye, so Cherry put the icepack down and started throwing her things in the trash. She stood to thank Margaret for her kindness when the girl began to sing. "You bring restoration . . ."

Cherry froze. Margaret was saying something to her, but Cherry didn't hear her. She was drawn to the girl on the stage and the words she was singing. The pull was as forceful as a magnet's to metal. Cherry walked toward the stage before she even realized what she was doing. Familiar words tugged at her. They unlocked something from her past, and she began to sing.

"You've taken my pain, called me by a new name. You've taken my shame and in its place you give me joy." Tears flowed down her face unchecked as easily as the words flowed from her mouth. She knew this song. She'd sung it before in a church. It came from deep within her heart. She felt a serene calm come over her, a surge of real joy. She locked eyes with the girl onstage and felt a jolt pass through her whole body, an instant connection. Did she know her?

She looked around, frightened. Was anyone else aware of what was happening? That's when she saw it—HOPE. It popped up everywhere. A sign hung on the keyboard. It was written on the guitar the man played. He even had it tattooed on his forearm. Above the stage a banner read "Hope Ministries."

Her heart began to race uncontrollably. It was more than she could handle. She had to get out of there. It was too painful to remember all she'd lost, a life filled with joy and love. It was foreign now. She noticed Margaret heading her way and knew she couldn't stay one minute longer.

Cherry turned to run away as the girl singing ran off the stage. She'd almost made it out of the park when the girl screamed, "Wait! Don't leave! We want to help you."

CHAPTER 34

The words stopped her as if she'd run into a brick wall. "Help me? What do you know about helping me?" Cherry turned, raised her voice. "I couldn't walk away from my life, even if I wanted to." Cherry screamed at the girl.

"There's always hope. We can get the help you need to start a new life. Hope is not lost," the girl said. She stopped a few feet away. Margaret came and put her hand on the young girl's back. She looked at Cherry with those beautiful blue eyes. No judgment, no disgust, only love.

Recognition hit Cherry. It hurt to breathe. She knew this girl. She had sung that song before. With this girl.

"Sydney?" she whispered. She looked a little different, but it had to be Sydney. They were best friends. Before life took a tailspin. "Hope is lost," Cherry said. "She's been lost for over a year. Don't you get it, Sydney?"

Sydney stepped back as if she had been slapped.

"Hope left when hell came knocking at her door. Everything is different now. I'm different. Hope is dead and Cherry is all that's left. Just leave me alone. Get away from me. I don't want any of my filth to rub off on you."

Cherry turned to leave but Margaret stopped her. When Margaret's arms went around her, Hope clung to her as if she were a life preserver. Her body heaved out tears as all her pain and heartache reached the surface. She started to retch; Margaret helped her to a nearby garbage can and rubbed her back while she heaved.

"Let it out, sweetheart." Margaret held her tight, refusing to let go. Her own tears fell freely.

As Cherry stood up and continued to cry, she felt another set of arms come around her. They belonged to Sydney. The three of them huddled for a long time before anyone spoke. Several volunteers were glued to the scene unfolding before them, but they knew better than to step into the situation and overwhelm the young girl.

"Don't you understand, Hope? You're the reason I've been coming out here. Every time I sang a song or served food, it was like I was doing it for you."

Margaret led them inside a tent and sat them down. She put a blanket around Cherry to help her stop trembling—but the temperature had nothing to do with the tremors raging through Cherry's body.

"I don't know if you want me to call you Cherry or Hope," Margaret said, "but either way, you don't have to continue in that lifestyle anymore. We can get you out of here safely."

"I can't! T will hurt my mom. He always told me if I didn't do exactly what he said, he would kill her in front of me. I can't let him hurt my mom. I won't! She's the only good thing in my life. Not my mom!" Cherry sobbed hysterically.

Margaret patted Cherry's leg as she stood up. "Stay here with Sydney for a minute. I need to talk with someone. He's a detective, but he won't hurt you or lock you up. He'll know what to do." As Margaret walked off, Sydney tentatively reached out to take Cherry's hand.

In a few minutes Margaret returned with a man who looked familiar. Cherry wasn't sure where she'd seen him before, but she recognized him. Was he one of her johns? Was she being set up? Then it hit her—he was the man who had moved in down the hall a couple of weeks ago. He always seemed to watch her and T whenever they left the apartment. He made her feel nervous.

"Hey there. My name is Detective Johnson." He knelt in front of her. "I'm with the Atlanta Police Department. You might have seen me in your building."

"Yes, sir. You're a cop?" Cherry wasn't sure if she could trust him.

"I'm an undercover detective. I've been watching your building because we received tips about young girls seen in the company of older men on the premises. I had my eye on you but I couldn't do anything until I gathered enough evidence. It looks like you found your own way out."

"T left tonight without locking the door. He usually locks me in when he goes out, but he was in such a rage he forgot. I had to run."

"We're going to get you to safety. First, we need to make T think you've been arrested. I'll need your help to make it work, but I promise to keep you safe. Are you up for it?"

"As long as my mom is safe."

"Your mom will be fine. I've already sent a car after her. I'll head back to your building and call up to the apartment from the lobby phone. I won't say anything when T answers. He'll think it's you and want to know why you aren't upstairs. When I don't say anything, he'll come down, then I'll signal you to start across the front of the apartment building like you're coming in from a walk. I'll be in the lobby. We'll have another undercover officer on the street near you so you'll be completely covered. He won't be able to get close to you, I promise."

Cherry kept looking at her hands, twisting them nervously as he talked. It sounded like it might work.

"Once we know T sees you, an officer in uniform will pull up to the door and arrest you for prostitution. He'll rattle off a list of charges. T will see you in handcuffs. You'll need to fight back so it looks legit. He's not stupid. He's not about to come to your rescue. He'll assume you're being taken to lockup downtown, but instead we'll take you to a safe house and get you in a treatment program."

Detective Johnson paused, giving her time to process all he was saying.

"The only other thing you'll have to do is call him tomorrow morning, but it will be from a secure line. Tell him you're in jail and need him to bail you out. He'll disappear. He won't risk being connected to you. You'll be safe in treatment, and your mom will be out of harm's way. T will go back to business as usual, and with your testimony, we'll be able to lock him up for good. Are you willing to do it?"

Cherry sat stunned, before weighing her options. "Someone's on the way to get my mom now? I won't do anything until I know she's safe."

"Absolutely. The officer will bring her to the safe house so she can see you before we take you to a treatment center. We can let you talk to her. We'll keep watching T's every move. You have my word she'll stay safe."

"If I go back to him, he'll kill me." Cherry sighed. "I'll do it, but I need a pack of cigarettes."

Detective Johnson raised an eyebrow.

"He'll see them in my hand and think I've gone out for more. He knows how addicted I am."

Detective Johnson turned to Sydney. "You'll have to stay here. I know you want to help, but the best thing you can do for Hope is get back onstage and keep doing what you came down here to do. We'll let you know the minute Hope's secure. Don't tell anyone about what's happening. We need to keep this as quiet as possible until Hope is in the safe house, and her mom is secure."

The cell phone on Detective Johnson's belt beeped. He looked at it. "Your mom's en route, Hope."

"I want to hear her voice."

His phone beeped again. "Are you sure you want to talk to her before we do this?"

"Yes, sir. There's no point if she isn't safe."

Detective Johnson dialed his colleague and handed Hope the phone. It felt weird in her hand, hot against her ear, comforting.

"Mom?" Hope sobbed at the sound of her mom's voice. "I'm glad you're safe. I'll see you soon."

A hardness came over Hope as she handed the phone back to Detective Johnson. She stood tall and steeled herself. She took the money Detective Johnson handed her to buy a pack of cigarettes. With one more glance back at Sydney, she headed for the apartment building with an undercover officer trailing her.

The officer radioed Detective Johnson when they reached the building. "We're here, ready to go on your mark."

"I've been waiting a long time to lock up this scumbag. Let's do this thing."

Detective Johnson placed the call.

T hung up when no one responded. "Yeah!" Johnson dialed again.

"Cherry, is that you? Where the hell have you been? You better answer me, bitch. I'm in no mood for games. Stop messin' with me or you're gonna pay!"

The elevator began to descend. T had taken the bait. Hope was nervous, but she walked toward the door on Detective Johnson's signal.

Hope approached the big glass double doors to the apartment building as the elevator doors opened. T stormed out with a fury. His eyes were wild as he surveyed the lobby. Detective Johnson flipped through junk mail like it was his. Hope made her way up the stairs to the door. Just as T crossed the lobby, a police car screeched up with the lights flashing. T froze. Hope looked from T to the cops as they stormed her.

The cops pulled her hands behind her back and cuffed her. "Get your filthy hands off me!" She kicked and screamed. "I haven't done anything! You can't arrest me. Let me go! I know my rights! Let go of me, you pig!"

T turned to the mailboxes as if he didn't know her. The cops continued with the arrest. They read Cherry her rights. They put Cherry in the backseat of the patrol car. Through the window, she saw Detective Johnson throw the junk mail back into the trash and look up at T. They locked eyes for a moment before T walked back to the elevator.

The elevator doors closed and Detective Johnson walked outside. He climbed into an undercover car and smiled at the woman in the backseat. Amanda Ellis reached out to him, her bottom lip trembling.

"You did it. You found my baby."

He squeezed her hand as their car followed the patrol car carrying Hope to the safe house. He was so overcome with emotion, he couldn't speak. He nodded and held Amanda's hand. His own tears fell. He'd spent countless hours looking for Hope, even when the trail went cold. But it had been worth it. Amanda Ellis would finally have her daughter back.

Restoration
You bring restoration
You bring restoration
You bring restoration
to my soul

You've taken my pain
called me by a new name
You've taken my shame
and in its place, You give me joy

You take mourning and turn it into dancing
You take weeping and turn it into laughing
You take mourning and turn it into dancing
You take my sadness and turn it into joy

Hallelujah, Hallelujah
You make all things new, all things new

—Clay Edwards, Audra Hartke, and David Brymer

A LETTER FROM
SUSAN NORRIS

Dear Reader,

Thank you for taking the time to read *Rescuing Hope*. I know it wasn't an easy read. The commercial sexual exploitation of children is the fastest growing crime in the world today. It is estimated it will soon surpass the illegal sale of drugs and arms. Called the crime hidden in plain sight, sex trafficking is taking place all across our nation. It is found in wealthy communities and poor communities; black, white, Asian and Hispanic communities; in our cities and in rural America. It impacts every demographic imaginable. The average age of a girl entering the sex trade is between twelve and fourteen years old. The life expectancy of a girl in the sex trade is seven years. The girls being trafficked in the United States are predominately American children being bought and sold for another's financial gain.

The first step in fighting this heinous crime is to raise awareness, which is the purpose of *Rescuing Hope*. My prayer is for this book to become a catalyst for conversation among you, your children, and your friends. Pass it on to others to read and allow it to become a springboard into action. Find out how you can get plugged in at www.susannorris.org.

I recognize many of you may be angry about the way *Rescuing Hope* ended. T walked away, and it appears he will face no time for his crime. The reality is that law enforcement officers spend months, and in some cases years, building an airtight case against a pimp or ring of pimps before arresting them to ensure they will be locked up for a long time. The last thing they want to do is act too quickly, allowing the pimp to get off with a slap on the wrist or less, putting him back on the streets where he can relocate and continue to victimize. Become a voice for the Hopes in your community. Let your elected officials know this is an important issue to you, and you want them to equip your local law enforcement to fight this crime. Lobby for harsher penalties for the pimps and johns who perpetuate this crime. You can make a difference.

I would love to hear from you. You can find me on Twitter (@SusanCNorris) and Facebook (Susan Norris author), or email me at Susan@Susannorris.org. Raise your voice and make a difference for those who cannot be heard. You too, can become a voice for hope.

DISCUSSION STARTERS

With knowledge comes responsibility. *Rescuing Hope* is intended to be a catalyst for conversation between mothers and daughters, among youth groups, book clubs, and friends. Awareness comes from discussion, and building awareness is the first step in fighting this horrific crime. Here are a few questions to get you started:

- Before you read *Rescuing Hope* what did you think of when you heard the word *prostitute*? Has this book changed your opinion? If so, how?

- How did Troy make Hope feel responsible for the rape? How have you taken ownership of an action that wasn't your fault?

- Why do you think Hope was willing to cross the line and try marijuana? Have you ever encountered a situation that caused you to consider crossing a line you've stood firm on before? If so, explain.

- T gained information from Hope quickly and almost effortlessly. What steps do you take to protect yourself when talking with people you've just met? What about online?

- Why do you think it is easy for young girls to be deceived by a pimp?

- What steps did you see Sydney take to try and help Hope? Do you think you have to be an adult to be involved in fighting the issue of human sex trafficking? What are some things you could do today to get involved?

- What do you think happens to Hope once she is rescued? Do you think she will ever have the chance at a normal life? Explain.

These are just a few questions to get your discussion started. Keep the conversation going. Share your questions for discussion at Susan@susannorris.org.

GET INVOLVED

Remember, we need your voice, your gifts, and your talents in this fight for freedom and awareness. For more information on how and where to get involved, check out these front line organizations.

- **Wellspring Living**'s "mission is to confront the issue of childhood sexual abuse and exploitation through awareness, training, and treatment programs for women and girls. Wellspring Living's vision is to serve locally, influence globally."
www.wellspringliving.org

- **Out of Darkness** runs "a 24/7 hotline with volunteers trained to answer rescue calls. Those volunteers will then activate responders who are trained to make contact with and offer rescue to trafficking victims. Victims will be offered a safe place to stay until they can transition to appropriate restorative services."
www.outofdarkness.org

- **Resolution Hope** has a vision "to stop domestic minor sex trafficking and exploitation in the United States; to educate, inspire and call to action those who are willing to stand with us to bring this human rights violation to an end."
www.resolutionhope.org

- **"Not For Sale** fights human trafficking and modern-day slavery around the world. Through international work on the ground and in mainstream supply chains, we proactively target the root causes of slavery while engaging and equipping the movement for freedom." www.notforsalecampaign.org

- **A Future. Not A Past.** "Spearheaded by the nonprofit youthSpark (formerly known as the Juvenile Justice Fund), A Future. Not a Past. is a campaign to stop the prostitution of children. Our campaign addresses the issue through our four-tiered strategy of research, prevention, intervention and education." www.afuturenotapast.org

- **"Street GRACE** mobilizes community resources—financial, human and material—to help individuals and organizations effectively fighting CSEC through advocacy, prevention and restoration. It is the goal of Street GRACE to create a powerful movement that unites Christian churches with a wide array of public, private and non-profit entities in order to bring about the end of commercial sexual exploitation of children." www.streetgrace.org

- **"Polaris Project** is one of the leading organizations in the global fight against human trafficking and modern-day slavery. Named after the North Star "Polaris" that guided slaves to freedom along the Underground Railroad, Polaris Project is transforming the way that individuals and communities respond to human trafficking in the U.S. and globally." www.polarisproject.org

- **"NightLight** is an international organization committed to addressing the complex issues of commercial sexual exploitation through prevention, intervention,

restoration, and education. NightLight's mission is to do 'whatever it takes' to effect change within the global sex industry. Our local offices in Atlanta, Bangkok, Branson, and Los Angeles build relationships with victims of commercial sexual exploitation and those who are at-risk and provide hope, intervention, rescue, and assistance by offering alternative vocational opportunities, life-skills training, and physical, emotional, and spiritual development to those seeking freedom."
www.nightlightinternational.com

- "**The A21 Campaign** stands for Abolishing Injustice in the 21st Century. When confronted with the horrific statistics surrounding human trafficking, it is easy to agree on the fact that 'someone should do something.' The A21 Campaign was born when the decision was made to raise our hand and be that 'someone.' It was a decision of ordinary people who decided to take responsibility regarding the issue of human trafficking. Our website is full of resources that will equip you to raise your hand and become that 'someone' willing to do 'something' to help abolish injustice in the 21st Century."
www.thea21campaign.org